KARMA'S SPIRIT

MAGICAL MIDLIFE IN MYSTIC HOLLOW: BOOK THREE

LACEY CARTER   L.A. BORUFF   HELEN SCOTT

DEDICATION

To my cowriters, we've had a really rough year, but I'm so grateful to have you both at my side. It means the world to me.

We may not have magic powers, but your friendships are their own kind of magic.

ONE

Emma

"Everybody dance—"

"Rock your body—"

"Tonight is the night—"

I held up one hand while trying to keep control of my laughter. "Hang on, I think we're all singing different songs."

Howling is more like it, Buster said from Carol's lap.

My friends and I dissolved into giggles, with me barely able to keep my attention on the road. The old tabby had complained about our singing a couple of times already on the trip, but Carol had reassured us he was excited about being able to help. He was even a little proud when she'd told him we needed him for his excellent tracking abilities. So, him muttering about us, knowing deep down he was happy to be here, for some reason made the trip even more fun.

And yet, my merriment was tinged heavily by the knowledge that we were less than thirty miles from my old home. The home I lived in with my piece of crap nearly ex-husband for too many years to count. Yes, a road trip with my awesome friends was definitely lifting my spirits, but it wasn't enough to make me forget the disaster that waited for me at the end of our adventure.

A disaster I'd wanted to avoid forever. But what was that old saying? Eventually, the truth always comes out. It was something like that...

"Another cookie?" Deva asked from the backseat, and the grin on her face was full of mischief.

I eyed the cookies in her bag and tried not to sigh. Is that why I was having such a good time when I should be sweating and clenching the steering wheel like I was running from a bank robbery? Deva's magic treats?

"Deva, those snacks you gave us..." I glanced at her in the rearview mirror. "Maybe I should've waited until I wasn't driving."

She waved me off. "I swear, they aren't that strong. And besides, I'm watching. I'll help keep you on track."

Carol adjusted her knitting needles beside me as another song came on the radio. Beth leaned forward from the backseat and turned a familiar dance song up and started singing along. Carol dropped her hands, but the knitting needles still floated in front of her. After a few seconds, the floating needles began knitting to the rhythm of the song on the radio as we sailed down the highway. The click-clack of the needles hitting each other strangely added to the music instead of distracting from it. Which is when Carol pulled out all her dance moves. Of course, her hands were free to dance to the music because her magic kept the needles moving, and before I knew it, I was joining her with one-handed dance moves of my own.

"Do you remember this song?" Beth shouted from the back.

Deva laughed. "At the homecoming dance?"

And then I remembered too. We'd gone as a group and spent the whole night dancing like morons, not caring if everyone thought we were idiots. I'd felt so dang free that night. So, alive. And as I belted out the words, that old feeling came rushing back to me.

A van went past us, with all the teenagers inside waving and laughing. We'd been following each other for hundreds of miles. They'd stop at a rest stop and we'd get ahead, then a while later we'd stop and end up meeting up again on the interstate. They passed us again now as we danced, all of them laughing at us silly women. But none of us minded one bit. When we were their age, we drove a little too fast too, and maybe made some bad choices.

Heck, who was I kidding? Weren't we on our way to try to find the ex I'd turned into a toad? Yeah, I was a safer driver these days, but I definitely wasn't done making mistakes. Hopefully, I was starting to make better choices though. My mind flicked to Daniel, and I wondered for a second what he was up to while we were on our road trip.

Beside us, another van sped up and passed us. I glanced at them and saw a mom and dad in the front seat. Behind them, the kids had their windows rolled down. All of them looked excited, and it made me smile. My ex and I might not have had a happy marriage at all times, but I remembered when my son would unroll his window on the freeway because he loved the feeling of the wind on his face.

My throat felt a little tight as they drove off and disappeared around the curving freeway. This was one of those times where all the rough parenting moments faded away, and I just wanted a little kid to run up to me and hug me like I was their whole world.

And then I reminded myself of everything else that comes with it, of the diapers, the late nights, the cleaning up puke, the hours creating meals and helping with homework, everything that comes with having a kid, and that tight feeling slips away. I think of having a nice cup of tea with my friends, and not being interrupted. And actually, having a full night's sleep. And not worrying about where Travis was and what he was doing all the time because he was an adult now. Or at least I tried not to worry so much.

Being in my forties had its perks.

Not even five minutes later, we rounded a large curve, and I slowly hit my brakes, terrified of what I saw ahead of us, but worried I'd be struck from behind if I slowed too fast. The van of kids, now a ways in front of us, swerved to avoid a dark SUV going the wrong way on the interstate. But to my shock, the SUV just kept going, racing toward the van with the family in it just in front of us.

I wanted to cry out, but it was already too late.

The mom, who had been driving her children with dad in the passenger seat, must've jerked the wheel, because the huge vehicle tilted and rolled. I slammed on my brakes while the wrong-way SUV sailed past me at a horribly high speed.

My friends all screamed, sounds of terror and shock reverberating through our car and ringing in my head.

On the other side of the guard rail was a huge drop-off. Almost a cliff. If they went over that, who knew if any of them would survive? I could picture newspaper headlines I'd seen about that spot, and none of them had a happy ending.

Then, I pictured the family in my mind and felt cold dread rush through me. No, I couldn't let that happen. I couldn't let a family die in front of me if I could help it.

Without really thinking about what I was doing, I threw up my hands as the van rolled again, toward the embankment on the right, stretching my karmic magic out. I slowed the rolling of the van with my magic, pulling on the van as hard as I could to keep it from flipping again. Even though in the back of my mind, I was sure its momentum was too much for my magic to stop. Not in time, anyway.

But I knew I had to try.

This deep sense of something inside of me yanked hard, but not quite tearing. It was an uncomfortable sensation that bordered on painful, and then there was a familiar awareness as every hair on my body stood on end. If this was my first time using my magic, no doubt the feeling would have distracted me, letting that van roll just enough to send them over the edge. But I gritted my teeth and focused on what I was doing.

And to my shock, I managed to stop the vehicle. On all four wheels, like something out of a cartoon, although it was still crumpled and battered. A loud boom sounded behind me, along with the crunch of metal on metal, but when I glanced in my rearview mirror, all I could see was smoke, and a few cars that had screeched to a halt.

"Everyone okay?"

No, Buster grumbled. And I looked back to see him, all his hair standing on end, still in Carol's lap.

"He's fine," Carol said, a little breathless.

Time to move.

When we jumped out of the car, I looked back to find the SUV had slammed headfirst into the barrier between the interstates. My gut told me that this was bad. That a lot of people were going to be gravely hurt today, and I froze for one second, not sure who to go to first.

Then, a cool calm washed over me. The SUV would

have to wait. The family had to be seen to first. As I raced toward the minivan, I had a moment of wondering if all parents had this superpower. Could we all keep our heads during a crisis, so we didn't scare the kids?

We made it to the passenger door to see the dad unbuckling his seatbelt and struggling to get to the back. Carol yanked open the sliding door on the side, which was so bent in she surely added a bit of *oomph* to it to get it to open without the jaws of life.

Six children stared at us with wide, scared eyes.

I climbed halfway into the car. "Is everyone okay?"

Please, let them be okay, I thought, as my gaze darted around the vehicle. I took in the kids and the surroundings in a split second. Cheerios and a variety of other snacks covered most surfaces and juice boxes, and water bottles were scattered around as well, not to mention the stuffed animals that had landed in awkward positions across the seats.

"I think so," the mom said, her voice shaking, as she unbuckled and turned in her seat. Her eyes were wide with fear, and I knew that there was the potential for her to go into shock, for all of them to go into shock really, but I also didn't think that the parents would until they knew the kids were okay.

We began the careful process of checking all the children over as sirens in the distance told us help was on the way. They looked scared. A little sore. But no one was bleeding. Nothing appeared broken.

It was almost a miracle. Or Karma had done more than just stop them from going over the edge. I wasn't really sure.

As soon as we knew nobody in the van was grievously injured, we turned almost as one and hurried toward the SUV to find a woman passed out. As I assessed the situation, I waved the others. on to check on any other cars that had been involved. She'd hit her head, probably on the steering wheel. No airbag had deployed.

Damn it.

Her limp hand fell to the side, displaying a diabetes medical alert bracelet.

My stomach turned, and my eyes prickled with tears. "Can you hear me?" I yelled. I'd been angry, but it seemed like she was having a diabetic emergency. I'd heard stories about how easy it could be to mix up the two at first sight.

I grabbed the woman's shoulder and leaned into the car... and a large, nearly empty plastic bottle of vodka fell out from beside her. The red and silver label glinted in the light as though it was mocking the whole situation. My gaze was glued to that bottle as I tried to make sense of what I was seeing.

She moaned and moved her head. Her eyes fluttered open, but her gaze wouldn't focus on my face. "I'm not drunk. Just had... a couple."

A sigh slipped from my lips. My guess was this wasn't her first rodeo, which was sad in so many ways. Her bad choice could've had a very different outcome today. Now though, she'd live. Hopefully with one hell of a headache and a lot of jail time.

I turned back to see the ambulance pulling up and spotted a sign on the other side of the van I hadn't noticed before.

As Carol, Beth, and Deva came to my side they noticed my gaze locked on to the sign as I sighed.

Welcome to Springfield.

"Well, that can't be a good omen," Deva muttered.

She was right. If this was how my trip home was starting, I wondered how it would end...

TWO

Emma

The sun set behind the road as we left the flashing lights behind us. "Whoa," I muttered. Exhaustion crawled over my skin and seeped into my bones as we started to drive away. I was more than a little thankful that the bulk of the trip was over. Now we just had to get to my old house within the city.

"Whoa is right." Deva shook her head sadly. "I didn't bring enough snacks to lift us out of this kind of mood."

I wasn't sure there *were* enough snacks to lift us out of this funk. We'd sat by the curb as the ambulance had loaded the drunk driver up. As they did, another one had pulled up and the paramedics started checking the children out. While everyone spoke to the police, we tried to cheer the children up. We played random games, talked to them about school, about the family trip they were on, anything to distract them from what had just happened, and how scared they were. We each told them about our kids as well, I told them all about how Travis hated road trips because he'd get so bored in the car and couldn't read or anything because he got car sick. They were appropriately horrified on Travis' behalf.

Once the police had finished taking the parents' statement, we waved goodbye to the kids and their parents, all of whom still looked shaken. It was our turn to give our statements. Of course, it went without saying that we left out the magical assistance I'd given the van. That wasn't something I particularly wanted to admit to, and since it wasn't something they'd believe anyway it seemed safer and smarter all around to just omit that detail.

Now we were finally back on track, without the fun and frivolity of before the wreck. "Hey," I said brightly. "Nobody died, and if we hadn't been there, more than likely they would've."

"True." Carol nodded decisively. "We saved the day." She glanced at me, then amended her statement. "You did. It wasn't us that stopped that van like that." The relief in her voice was almost palpable and I felt the exact same way. Just the thought of what would have happened to that family in the minivan was enough to make me nauseous.

I shrugged and tried to push it from my mind as I turned onto the exit that the drunk driver had most likely come up. It was the only way they could have gone to get on our side of the interstate unless they were off-roading, but there were no signs of that, none of the grass had tire treads and there wasn't any mud on the side of the road. My dampened mood elevated slightly, but not too happy.

Nervous.

Anxious.

Slightly terrified.

"Oh, geez," I said. "I still don't see how this is going to work. Surely Rick and Candy have disappeared by now."

Beth blew air between her lips, and it curled upward

making her bangs wave. "Nah, we can do a location spell on them. We'll get this sorted out."

"But first, I need a glass of wine and a rest in a chair that isn't a car seat," Deva said, grimacing as she shifted in the backseat.

"Same," I muttered. "Maybe a bit of a walk." My hips and lower back were killing me. Whoever said road trips were fun was only right for so long, at some point they became a guessing game of how to sit so you can walk the next day and not have a bunch of back pain.

As I navigated the streets of Springfield, I thought about that drunk woman. She needed major help. Karma would want it. Somehow, I knew that she'd rather have the drunk woman get help than just pure punishment. And maybe something good would come out of this for that little family, too. I knew I'd appreciate Travis more if I almost lost him like that. It wasn't that I didn't love and appreciate him now, but there's nothing like a near-death experience to drive that point home. Silver linings and all that.

Buster stretched from Carol's lap as soon as I put the car in park in front of my house. It looked quiet... lonely. Bringing my friends here felt like I was seeing it again for the first time, only this time everything looked like there was something off about it. The cedar siding had already needed to be repainted and in the few weeks I'd been gone it had only gotten worse with paint flecks littering the ground in places. One of the shutters was a bit crooked and I wondered if it had been damaged in a recent storm. The flower beds were overgrown and in need of a good weeding and though the curtains were drawn it was like you could see the state I'd left everything in inside, and though I didn't remember it clearly, I had the sneaking suspicion it wasn't good. The whole place had a forlorn air to it.

"This is not a happy house," Deva said as she leaned forward from the back seat to peer up at the house. "Lots of bad memories there. You need to get it sold and move on with your life so a new family can start making better memories in it. Maybe we should sage it." She spoke as though the building itself had memories, and for all I knew maybe it did, but I hoped whoever ended up buying it didn't get infected with my bad marriage or something. I truly wanted someone to be happy in that house. I just knew it could have never been me, not for long at least.

"There are good memories though, too," I said. "Travis grew up here. All my memories of his childhood are painted with the backsplash of this place." I sucked in a deep breath and got out of the car. "Let's see how bad of shape I left the house in." I didn't remember details, but I'd been pretty low before leaving town. I probably left dishes in the sink and garbage overflowing. "I hope it doesn't stink," I muttered.

Carol chuckled. "That's what magic is for." I wanted to ask more about that, I mean I knew she could knit without needing to hold the needles, but could she do things like vacuum without actually vacuuming herself? If so, this was going to be a major breakthrough in how I did my house-work, provided I could make any of that magic work for me. Knowing my luck though karma wouldn't lift a finger to help me do the dishes.

When I unlocked the front door and stepped inside, no stink overwhelmed me. There weren't critters running around, destroying everything. "So, far so good." The fact that there was no smell made me more nervous than I expected.

I stepped into the living room, but then furrowed my brows. "It's clean."

"Well, you left it in better shape than you thought," Deva said.

"No, I didn't."

One of Travis's shirts had been slung over the back of the recliner. "Oh, Travis has been here."

"There you have it. He's cleaned up."

That wasn't like him, but stranger things had happened under heaven and earth.

I moved toward the kitchen to find it spotless except for a coffee cup. I touched the side. Still warm. "Someone is here."

"Mom?"

I whirled to find Travis standing in the doorway, staring at me with nothing but boxer shorts on. "Hey, Pumpkin. I didn't know you were here."

A woman peeked her head around him. "Hi," she said in a small voice. Travis stepped to the side, and a tiny slip of a woman stepped into the kitchen. She wore a long, flowing mustard color skirt that had a flowery pattern to it and a creamy peasant blouse. Her golden blonde hair may as well have had a flower crown woven through it. It didn't though, instead she wore a headband that was turquoise with a pink pattern on it that had threads of gold woven in at some places making it sparkle whenever she turned her head.

At least she was dressed, unlike my son.

"Mom, this is Jacqueline." He smiled at the girl and the sun shined in his eyes. *Uh-oh.* He was head over heels. And she looked like she was about the furthest thing from who I'd pick for him. He was such a straight-laced kid and Jacqueline was... boho. That was a good word for it. She looked like she was into crystals and tarot and all that without actually knowing any of it might be real. I could imagine her saying that she wanted to go be one with the forest or something. Not that it was a bad thing, just not what I expected for my nerdy boy. But then, she was in the engineering program, too... maybe they had more in common than I thought.

Deva jumped forward and held out her hand as I stared at my son and his friend in shock. "Hello," she said. "I'm Deva, one of Emma's friends. It's so nice to meet you both." She dropped her voice but could barely keep the laughter from it as she added, "Maybe you want to run and put some clothes on?"

Travis's cheeks colored as he blinked rapidly, then jumped and ran out of the room. The familiar thump of his feet hitting the stairs at top speed made me smile and knocked me out of my musing. He'd run upstairs like that for most of his life, after school, after soccer, after his first girlfriend broke up with him, after me and Rick started fighting. My mood soured at the thought of my ex, but I wasn't going to let it ruin my first time meeting Jacqueline.

"So," I said brightly. "You're dating my son?"

Jacqueline looked at me with bright, worried eyes, as though she was expecting a full interrogation of some kind. It made me wonder what her previous boyfriends had been like, or if she was hiding something that she didn't want me to find out about. Or maybe her previous boyfriends' mothers had been unpleasant.

I shook my head a little to shake away the thought. Not everyone was suspicious and mysterious. This wasn't Mystic Hollow, after all.

THREE

Daniel

THE WOLF PACK was in trouble. *Again.*

"So, you paying the damages?" Sam rolled a toothpick between his teeth as he waited for me to answer, although I could see it in his face that he was already expecting me to reach for my checkbook, like I had a thousand times before. "I figure it's about five hundred for me to replace that table and the two chairs."

I glanced over at the members of the pack, sitting sullenly in cuffs. My hand went to my back pocket, ready to pull out my wallet. But for some reason, I hesitated. Was I doing these kids any good by always bailing them out? Ever since Thomas died, I'd been helping them out of trouble every time they managed to get themselves in these situations. I'd seen Nathan, Thomas's son, and the new head of their pack, hurting the same way I was hurting. But instead of keeping busy and trying to help this town the way I had,

Nathan just seemed to be leading himself and the rest of his pack to complete destruction.

Yes, I'd thought by this point things would be getting better. But judging by the boys' torn, dirty clothes and faces full of bruises, things weren't getting better. And maybe it was my fault. As a bear, I couldn't lead their pack or tell them what to do, but I could stop enabling them. Something I should have done a long time ago, a decade ago when he died. I didn't know if it was seeing Emma that had brought this desire for change inside of me, but regardless of the cause, I couldn't go down this road any longer.

It wasn't healthy. Not for me. Or for them.

"No." I drew my hand away from my money as the alpha, Nathan, looked up at me in shock. "Not this time."

Even Sheriff Samuel's eyebrows went up. But I looked away from his surprised expression to the boys. I could see it in Nathan's face. In all his twenty-something years, he'd never been in a situation that this old bear, or his father, didn't step up and bail him out of. I hoped, even if he hated me after this, he one day realized that I did him a favor.

God, I hope I was doing them all a favor.

His father would've been disappointed in me for being so soft with them. Yeah, he hadn't ever let Nathan get hurt, but he also didn't coddle him the way I had. He was preparing him every day of his life to become the next alpha. He taught him right and wrong. He helped him to grow up healthy and strong. And then... then he was gone and the solid foundation he'd built crumbled.

It wasn't all my fault. But I hadn't helped. And as Nathan's gray eyes met mine and narrowed in utter hatred, I felt my stomach twist. I loved this kid like he was my own, but if he had to hate me to learn to be better, then I'd accept this.

I looked at Sheriff Samuel, willing myself not to feel like a traitor. "Put them in lockup. They need to learn a lesson because this shit isn't getting any better."

The other wolves shuffled around and glared at me, and a feeling of betrayal and a whole lot of anger rolled off of them. It made me feel bad to see these lost kids probably feeling like they were losing another father figure. But if I was going to try my best to help them, then I needed to learn the difference between helping them and enabling them. By the end of this, they'd either improve, stay the same, or get worse, but at least I *tried* to make things better.

"If they can come up with the money to pay the damages, I can probably get them off with just community service," the sheriff said, adjusting the brim of his big cowboy hat, his mouth drawn into a thin line. No doubt he was thinking about how he was going to keep this rough pack of kids in our small jail until things got sorted out.

His gaze met mine, and he huffed, his belly protruding even further as he realized what I already knew. They didn't have the money. They couldn't put two and two together long enough to make any money. The lot of them were aimless. Not hunting the way the pack had done in the past, providing meat and fur to sell in the local shops, nor using the other resources on their lands to keep the pack coffers full.

It was kind of depressing. It wasn't that long ago that the wolves were comfortably wealthy, run like a well-oiled machine, and were something to be proud of. Damn it. They'd fallen so far, and where was I? Just putting one foot in front of the other, trying to ignore my broken heart? A fat lot of help that had done this pack.

Nathan's glare hit me again, and I swear he wanted to tear my head off. Wolves were known for being hot-headed, but most shifters knew when to bow their head and take their licks. Losing his dad so young had made Nathan angry. Bitter. And not at all the kind of man who sat up tall, accepted the consequences of his actions, and tried to better himself.

Maybe a little tough love would help the kid. Bailing him out certainly hadn't been doing it.

Without another word or even a backward glance, I walked out of the bar and got into my truck. Turning the key in the ignition, her loud engine roared to life, and I buckled up, hands shaking ever so slightly. Nathan's face kept flashing in my mind, but I put my pickup in drive and headed out of that dark parking lot.

I needed some time to myself. To clear my head. And not run back there, waving my wallet.

So, I did the only thing I could think of, I headed up into the mountains, driving my truck as far as the road went before getting out and shifting into my bear form. The shift only took a moment as my bones cracked and my larger body took shape. But the second I was in my more natural form, some of the weight of what I'd done fell off my shoulders. I allowed my thoughts to drift a bit as I focused on the sights and scents of nature. Green life. Small animals. Dirt. And water, close by. I breathed it all in, huffing like the old bear I was.

The walk helped me clear my head. Wolves were roaming the woods under the moonlight, too, but they left me alone. Technically this was the edge of their territory, but it had practically become my territory since Thomas had died. It was sort of our spot, so now I'd found myself returning here every time I felt lost.

Growing up, we'd hung out here a lot, learned the limits of our shifting. Ran and fought. Came here after breakups or when our parents were too much for us. It felt like this place was more home sometimes than my quiet cabin. They said home was where the heart was, right? Well, this place was what I associated Thomas with the most. And while it'd hurt too much to visit some of the places Sarah and I had gone together, this place managed to bring me peace instead of pain.

As I broke from the forest, I shifted back into my human form and walked the rest of the way on bare feet. The big red rock stuck out from the rest of the forest, so big the whole pack could have sat here with ease. I walked along the thick stone, listening to the way my feet slapped against it, and how the crickets and other night animals called to one another, not missing a beat, even when I moved among them. When I got to the edge, I could see more woods below me, and the ocean stretching out in front of me. The salty air whispered over my skin, and I shivered as goosebumps erupted along my naked flesh.

"Hey, Thomas," I said, my voice breaking a little. "I don't know what I'm doing, man."

I sighed and wished he was really here. "I met this girl. Well, re-met her. She's amazing. I never thought I'd find someone like Emma, especially not at our age." I chuckled sadly. "*My* age. But I did. And now I have to get the rest of me sorted out, so if she actually sees something with me too, I'm not too much of a mess to be the kind of man she needs."

My gaze swung to the place Thomas had always sat, and it was easy to pretend he was really here. Except that he would have bumped my shoulder and told me to not overthink it. To just enjoy Emma. To accept that it was okay that I was moving on and could see a future that wasn't lonely. But he wouldn't just say the words, he'd make me *believe them* so deep in my heart that I'd be sure I was on the right path.

That was something the lonely rock couldn't do for me.

"Emma has changed Mystic Hollow. Or maybe she's changed me, because I've realized I've been handling Nathan and the pack all wrong." I give a sad laugh. "But you already knew that didn't you? I bet if you could have screamed at me from the afterlife to pull it together, you would have."

The wind whistled around me in response.

"But I'm going to do better, I swear I will. Emma's been getting me back into police business, and I know it's been good for me. You would've told me I retired too early. That I'd be bored, but now I'm realizing it myself. That when you and Sarah died, I wasn't just trying to keep going until I could be with you. I'm still here, for a reason, and so I actually need to live a bit. Right?" I turned to where he always sat.

And I nearly fell off the rock. "Thomas!" I exclaimed. He was sitting there, looking at me with the world's saddest expression on his face. "How?"

I blinked, taking him in. It was him. Exactly the way I remembered him. Same gray eyes as Nathan, same light brown hair, and sharp lines to his face. Except, that he was bigger than his son. The only wolf to be nearly as big as me. And he was sitting next to me, glowing softly, a little transparent, but him.

It wasn't possible. Was it? I mean, I knew ghosts existed, but Thomas had been gone for a long time. There wouldn't be a reason for him to suddenly come back here. Would there?

I leaned forward and peered at him more closely, my voice wavering. "Thomas?"

His sad expression deepened, and my heart raced. If I accepted he was a ghost sitting with me now, I also needed to accept that he was here for a reason. And ghosts only crossed to the land of the living if it was important.

"Aren't you at peace?" I asked, my heart twisting at the thought that he hadn't achieved the peace I'd imagined in the afterlife.

After a second, he shook his head. Thomas opened his mouth, his lips moving but nothing coming out for several long seconds before his brows drew together and his shoulders slumped.

"Are you trying to tell me something?" I asked.

Thomas nodded enthusiastically.

"What is it?"

He moved his lips again, but nothing came out. If he was making any sounds in his realm, wherever he was, I couldn't hear them. And it made a growl tear from my throat. My best friend came all this way to tell me something, and I couldn't even hear him. How was that fair? How was any of this okay? Wasn't it enough that he'd died so early and so tragically? A car wreck, when he had a young son and at the same time as my Sarah's accident. It had been a horrible time of my life.

His face reflected the frustration I felt, and he reached out as if to touch my shoulder, but his hand went through me. In his face, I saw that there was something he desperately wanted to tell me. The sensation was so powerful that I felt the temperature around me drop and goosebumps erupted along my naked flesh.

"You need to tell me something important, but you can't. Or I can't understand you. Right?"

He nodded, and his eyes spoke volumes, that this was not something to be forgotten, and then he just faded away.

"Thomas!" I yelled and waved my hands around the area he'd just been moments before.

He'd been sad, upset, and definitely trying to tell me something. How could I get him back? "Thomas?" I whispered.

But he didn't return.

My thoughts spun. What could I do? How could I figure out what he wanted to say and give him peace? Was that even possible when he wasn't able to communicate his message?

I released a slow breath. I guess the best I could do is try to assume what he was trying to tell me. Maybe that would be enough for now.

"I'll do my best. I'll try to help your son, and whatever you were trying to warn me about, I'll look out for it, too."

But the tension in the air around me remained. Guessing wasn't enough. I had to know. I had to receive the message that Thomas had come back to tell me.

I stood, my hands bunching into fists. "I'll be back, Thomas. Try to show yourself again if you can."

With one last look at the breathtaking views off the cliff and down across the mountains, I turned and shifted, lumbering down the trail toward my truck.

If nothing else, it was good to see my old friend. For now. And I might just be an old bear, but old bears were stubborn. I'd figure out a way to communicate with my friend. You could count on that.

FOUR

Emma

"HONEY?" I offered, smiling at Jacqueline as I lifted the little jar.

Even though she smiled as she took the container of honey, the mood in the room was still incredibly tense as we sipped the tea I'd made while Travis dressed. I'd never really given my son permission to have a girl here, especially not without me being home. And he certainly hadn't asked.

But I wanted to make a good impression. And I also knew deep down that Travis was an adult, and I didn't want to treat him like a child. He was a man now, and my little man had a new girlfriend. It might be a little hard to wrap my brain around, but I wouldn't risk alienating him by making this whole thing into a bigger deal than it was.

Besides, even if I didn't know if the relationship was destined to be long-term, I didn't want to get off to a bad start with the girl on the off chance she ended up being my daughter-in-law or having my grandchildren.

Whoa. Okay, that was a whole other thing. I must be really flustered to be jumping between trying to remember my son was an adult, and suddenly imagining him married with kids. I needed to take a deep breath, keep smiling, and try not to say anything too stupid.

Yeah, I could get through this one situation without putting my foot in my mouth. Right?

Ugh. I wasn't sure. So, I reached for my tea and took a big drink, hoping to buy myself some time.

"So," Jacqueline said, a small smile twisting her lips. "Are you guys witches?"

I choked on my tea.

"What?" Deva said in a high-pitched voice.

I started coughing out the warm drink while Beth patted my back, all our gazes locked on the young woman across from us. Grabbing a napkin from the table, I patted my mouth, took a few deep breaths, then looked at my friends. This was all pretty dang new to me. Should we just treat her like she's crazy? Confess? Jump on my old broomstick, cackle, and fly off?

Carol gave a grin that was so forced it was painful to look at. "Who, us?"

We all laughed, and there was no way Jacqueline didn't know how tense and uncomfortable we were. But I didn't care, my gaze kept sweeping to where my broom was in the pantry in the kitchen. I'm sure the others knew how to fuel the thing and get us out of here. Or maybe there was a spell we could hit her with? Or was bespelling your son's new girlfriend a no-no even for witches?

Jacqueline raised her arm and showed us a tattoo on her arm. It was a very specific Wiccan symbol. More complicated and beautiful than any I'd seen before, with dark lines on the outside, and tiny lines and symbols within the symbol. Whoever had tattooed the thing was a true artist, and I wasn't usually a fan of tattoos.

When none of us responded, she said, "I'm a witch, too."

That was the moment Travis chose to come back into the room. He seemed to have caught the tail end of our conversation because he chuckled. "I don't know about Mom's new friends, but she's just a regular mom. No witchy stuff going on here."

"Besides, witches don't really exist! That's stuff for Halloween!" I said, smiling brightly, my gaze begging the girl to drop the conversation.

"The tattoo is nice," Deva began slowly, "but maybe you could tell us more."

To my surprise, Jacqueline nodded as Travis took the seat next to her. "Witches run in my family line. For the most part, all the women in our family have the gift, although my brothers have a few unique abilities that would make them weaker warlocks."

Deva and Carol exchanged a look, and then Carol asked, "what kind of witch are you?"

Jacqueline grinned. "Well, I can do a lot of things, but mostly, my specialty is music. I can play any instrument and sing nearly any song. And through my music, I can make people feel the way I want. That's why one of my minors is music."

I looked at my friends. She did sound an awful lot like a witch, but they'd be the ones to know for sure.

"I haven't met a lot of music witches," Deva said, and some of the tension in the room eased a bit.

Travis laughed. "I know, I know, it sounds weird, but you guys don't need to humor her. She really is a witch. Not the kind you see in movies and tv, doing cruel spells and hurting people. What she can do is really... beautiful. And cool. I didn't believe it until she played for me, and I felt it. That's a kind of magic that's real." His gaze swung to hers, and there was so much love in his eyes that it distracted me for a second.

"We understand—" Deva began, but Travis cut her off.

"No, this isn't drugs, or some new young person thing," his grin was a little smug.

"Travis, they believe us. They're witches too," Jacqueline said, then looked at me to confirm her words.

Travis's gaze swung to me, and his smug grin fell away, and his mouth dropped open. I glanced at my friends trying to see if they would object to me telling him the truth. If there was anyone who deserved to know it was him. When I didn't see any of them glaring at me or shaking their heads I decided to forge ahead.

"Err." I set my teacup down and sighed. "There's something I have to tell you."

Travis stared at me with his eyebrows up. "Don't tell me you've been hiding being a witch from me all my life, because there's just no way..."

I held up my hand and shook my head. "No, no. Not that. Before I left town, I saved an older lady from being hit by a car. It turned out she was Karma, with a capital K. And now I have her powers."

"Karma like... I cheat on you so the next girl cheats on me. Or I help someone, and then I win the lottery, karma?"

I nodded.

"So, you have superpowers...?"

"Kind of," I said softly, "but my friends are regular witches"

Travis stared at me with his mouth slightly open, and I could feel his thoughts turning. I tried to remember what it was like when I was just human, and all of this stuff was new to me. A lot of it had been unbelievable. But then again, if he'd accepted his girlfriend was a real witch, this wasn't his first time stepping into this world. So, he could accept that magic was real. But could he accept me like this? My heart froze, worried he'd reject me or hate the thought of me having powers.

But then he grinned. "That is so cool!"

Deva, Carol, and Beth burst out laughing. "Well, that was nerve-wracking," Deva said.

"Ever since Jacqueline and I started dating, I've been..." He glanced at her and grinned. "Well, my eyes have been opened."

"That's wonderful, honey," I said and patted his hand, still feeling nervous.

To my surprise, he turned his hand around and held mine. "I know sometimes you were worried I'd end up too much like dad."

"I never said that!" I rushed out.

He squeezed my hand. "You didn't have to. I saw the fear in your eyes sometimes when you tried to hide it. But I want you to know that even though I can be a bit—"

"Straight-laced?" Jacqueline offered with a laugh.

He looked back at her with a smile that filled his eyes. "Yes. And I am. But I'm also the kind of person who knows how to bring happiness, excitement, and change into my life." Then, Travis looked back at me. "And it seems that when you got rid of Mr. Buzzkill, you found your own happiness and excitement too."

"I have," I said. "These ladies... are amazing." I choked a bit on my words. "And my life in Mystic Hollow has become more than I ever imagined life could be."

"Good, you deserve that," he said.

I smiled. "And if Jacqueline brings that into your life, you deserve her too."

Chatty humans haven't set down a food bowl yet, Buster growled.

Jacqueline jumped. "Your cat... it talked." Then, her eyes widened. "One of you is an animal witch."

Beth lifted a hand. "Guilty!"

"That's... awesome!" Jacqueline squealed.

"I didn't hear anything," Travis said with a frown.

Deva laughed. "Don't worry, you're not missing much. Buster is a grumpy tabby."

You'd be grumpy too after being stuck in a car with howling humans, Buster grumbled.

Everyone except Travis laughed.

"I guess there's been a lot of changes, for both of you," Deva said, nodding between Travis and me.

His smile faltered. "Well, there are more changes than just me having a girlfriend."

My gaze swings to her belly. Is she pregnant? If she's pregnant, I need to react correctly.

I feel a giant forced smile twist my face as my brain screams *nooooo*, and my mouth forms the word *congratulations*, but luckily for me, Travis keeps talking before the word can leave my lips.

"Here's the thing. We applied for a study abroad program that neither of us got into. It was a really great opportunity, so we were bummed. But two people dropped out at the last second, so Jacqueline and I were offered their spots," Travis said. "We had to take the spots right away or they would've gone to someone else. We said yes, but I didn't want to leave without talking to you. Today we were actually packing. We planned to come to Mystic Hollow and tell you the news."

"Study abroad?" My mind went to war-torn countries, shady back alleys, and all the other scary things I'd seen on the news.

"To Europe," he said with a grin. "Jacqueline's getting more art classes, and I'm getting to knock out most of my elective classes in one shot."

Europe. Meaning... tea, crumpets, fairy circles, and corner markets? Right? Okay, breathe, I could handle that.

I realized everyone was staring at me, so I squeezed his hand again. "Oh, honey, that's wonderful," I said in my sweetest, most supportive voice. And I did support him, but the thought of my little boy going overseas without me still made my toes curl.

But he wasn't my little boy anymore. Something I needed to keep reminding myself. "When do you leave?" I asked.

"Three days. But we were going to go back to the school and say goodbye to our friends and stuff."

Three days? Three days?

Unable to help myself, I leaned over and squeezed him in a tight hug. He hugged me back and whispered, "I love you," against my hair.

"I love you too."

"But you're really going to be okay, right? I know things were rough with the divorce, so I can make sure to call you more, and—"

I pulled back from him, whipping a traitorous tear from my cheek. "I'm the mom! You don't have to worry about me! I'll worry about you every second until you get back, so you make sure to live it up there."

"And I'll look after him," Jacqueline said softly.

I reached over and squeezed her hand. "Thank you, sweetie."

Something in her eyes made my heart ache. It was like until that moment she wasn't sure where we stood. And maybe it was because with all the witch stuff, I wasn't sure where we stood. But now I knew. No matter what happened with their relationship, as long as she was tied to my son, I would try to treat her like my child too. With love and respect.

Love, kindness, and respect cost nothing at all.

"But you make sure to take care of yourself too. Okay? And when you guys get back, I'll take you out to dinner, to hang out on the beach, and you guys can show me all the photos from your big adventure."

"I'm sure I'll post stuff online," Travis said with a snort of amusement.

"Of course," I replied with a smile. I'd just have to remember to check.

I released them both, and the conversation turned to cautious questions about what my powers were, and what my friends could do, and what we were getting up to in Mystic Hollow. I almost told them about our crime-fighting life, but realized it would probably make Travis worry more, and he didn't need anything else to worry about right now. And then, we asked questions about their school, how they met, and about Jacqueline's family. Time ticked away, and the conversation began to die away as we settled into a tired comfortableness.

Then, Jacqueline went to take a shower. I wandered into Travis's room and smiled at his old band posters and the trophy from the chess tournament he won. The room was full of boxes labeled with his and Jacqueline's names. "Sorry for bringing it all here," he said. "But this all happened really fast."

"It's okay." I watched him pack a suitcase and smiled. "I

think you and Jacqueline are a good match." I meant it, too. At first, I hadn't seen it, but the more I observed them together, the more I liked them together. They were different, sure, but why would that be a bad thing? They might just complement each other.

After giving him a hug, I returned to the kitchen, where my girls had switched the tea out for wine.

Travis and Jacqueline came down a few minutes later with duffel bags and backpacks. "We'll be back for the last of our stuff and to officially say goodbye the day after tomorrow," Travis said. "In the meantime, will you be here?"

I nodded. "Most likely. We're going to pack some of my stuff and close down the house. It'll be here when you get back if you want to stay here."

Travis smiled at me. "If you decide not to hang onto it, just toss my stuff in a storage bin. Don't let my stuff be the reason to hang onto the past."

Darn it. This kid was too smart for his own good.

"Thanks. Drive safely."

After I closed the door behind them, I leaned against it and tried not to be sad that my baby was in college and going to study abroad. This was a good thing for him.

"It'll be good to get him out of town," Deva said. "Maybe he won't get mixed up in all this mess."

I stiffened, remembering why we were here and about my stupid ex.

"Agreed," I said and accepted a glass of wine from Beth. "And I vote we look for my asshole ex-husband in the morning. Tonight is for us and for wine." Hopefully I wouldn't be too hungover tomorrow to deal with this mess.

FIVE

Emma

Something about waking up in this house made me unsettled. Being back home had been good for my soul. I didn't like being back here, despite the good memories of my son the house held.

As much as I might not admit it to anyone else, the bad memories were more potent. I was trying my best to remember the good times, to focus on Travis growing up here and all the joy that had come along with having my son, but everything felt shadowed by the pain of the memories with Rick.

My ex was a virus that infected everything he touched. Though I never would have had Travis without Rick, obviously, I couldn't help but wish the memories I had with my son weren't tainted with Rick's selfishness. Fortunately, Travis himself seemed to have dodged that personality trait bullet. I would give anything for my son, I'd even do all of this over again, knowing the pain I would go through, just to have him and the joy and happiness he'd bring to the world. It was that joy and happiness that had kept me going for so long, even on my darkest days, and it was that reason I'd been reluctant to get rid of the house.

Travis was right though, as usual, I had photos and videos to keep those memories, and didn't need to keep the house, not when I now realized how bad it made me feel. The fact that Travis had recognized that and was encouraging me to get rid of the house wasn't surprising, the boy was too observant for his own good. I wasn't sure where he got that from because clearly, I'd missed quite a bit if my marriage had fallen apart, and I hadn't been able to stop it.

No, that wasn't fair. The marriage wasn't just on me. I wasn't the only one who could have made it work. Rick could have tried as well. He could have talked to me, but he didn't, instead, he chose another woman over me. Ugh. Did he have to be such a stereotype?

As I stretched, my nose and brain finally connected to one another, and I smelled coffee. Oh, yum. If Deva made it, it'd have a special pick-me-up and put me in a peppy good mood for the day. When I listened carefully, I heard the murmur of voices downstairs and figured I was probably the last one up.

My old self would have been horrified. The guests were up before me and making their own coffee and who knew what else? Unacceptable.

A thought occurred to me as I pushed my ridiculous old hang-ups from my mind that they might have been able to send the coffee smell up here somehow to wake me. I'd have to ask about that at some point. There was still so much I didn't know about witchy stuff.

"This house is heavy," Carol said by way of greeting when I walked into the kitchen thirty minutes later. I'd taken a quick shower and hadn't even bothered to blow dry my hair, today I was just letting it do whatever it wanted.

There was no reason to get all spiffy and I definitely wasn't going to put the effort in when I knew we were going to be searching for toads. Who knew what we'd be getting into? Still, it'd taken me 30 minutes to get myself together enough to come downstairs.

"Heavy?" I thought I knew what Carol meant, but I wanted to make sure. As Deva reached across the table to hand me a cup of her phenomenal coffee, I smiled gratefully. She must've brought the ingredients with her because I doubt I had anything that could, or should, be used to make coffee.

"You were unhappy here," Beth said, her blue eyes tinged with sadness and her expression and body language muted from her normal bubbly self. "We can feel it. Sleeping here, it's like the unhappiness melted into me."

Guilt twinged in me. Maybe we should have sprung for a hotel? I sighed and looked around. "I can't deny I felt it, too. Not as much as you guys probably did with your witchy powers, but yeah. It's there." I don't know if I would have even noticed it, or if I did notice it understood what I was feeling if it weren't for my friends. Maybe it was partly because of the whole karma thing as well, but I was definitely more aware of the way sadness seemed to cling to the very air in the house.

After a sip of coffee and another sigh, this one happy, I looked at the plate Deva set in front of me. "This looks amazing." She seemed to have found her way around the kitchen without any issue and was definitely putting her talents to good use.

The plate held an egg-white omelet with feta, spinach, tomatoes, and even some artichoke if my eyes weren't deceiving me. There must have been a decent amount of spices in there as well because it smelled like I'd died and gone to heaven. I dug in with a moan and enjoyed what was probably the first meal I'd eaten in this kitchen that I hadn't cooked or ordered myself. I couldn't believe how my friends were taking care of me, even here, in my unhappy house.

"I took a quick trip to the store," Deva said, giving me a wink.

Even though they didn't have the cat food I like, grumbled Buster from a corner of the kitchen, where he was glaring at his food bowl.

Deva laughed. "Don't worry, we'll be back home soon." She shivered. "And out of this house."

I tried to ignore the wave of guilt that swept through me. "I don't think this kitchen has ever seen food cooked this good. Heck, I don't remember the last time this place was filled with friends and laughter."

"You didn't have a lot of friends here?" Beth asked, stirring her coffee.

I shrugged. "I had friends, but no one like you guys. I guess I convinced myself that just calling you guys and video chatting with my brother constantly was enough. That it was okay if most of my relationships here felt... like surface relationships. Like, I'm friends with someone because they're friends with Rick, or because So-and-So was the mom of one of Travis's friends. It wasn't until I went back to Mystic Hollow that I realized just how much I missed being with people I could be myself with."

"This is a good time for you to appreciate how your life has changed," Carol said. "Things are never going to be like that again."

Her words felt like a bell had suddenly been rung within my soul. She was right. Things were never, ever going to be like that again. I did hope that I was able to find Rick and Candace, but it was mainly because I knew once I did, they would be out of my life forever. Rick and I would be able to finalize our divorce and I could sell this place and finally, *finally*, cut all ties with Springfield and my ex.

"Maybe adding a date with someone new?" Deva added slyly, pulling me from my thoughts. She knew darn well Daniel and I had talked about it.

I couldn't stop the blush from creeping up my cheeks. I was looking forward to that date. Could it even really be called a date though? I supposed I'd have to wait and see. I had no idea what Daniel had in mind, but it had very obviously been a while since I'd been single, and I wasn't sure I even knew how to date anymore. Those were worries for another time though.

"What about you?" I asked Carol, trying to take some of the heat off myself. "Ready for a new outlook?"

She shrugged and didn't quite meet my eyes. She hadn't moved on from the love of her life, Bryan, and didn't apparently want to talk about it. I wish I knew about what had happened between them, what had made her completely shut herself off from even dating anyone else? I could barely remember him; the memories were distorted by time and pregnancy brain. In all honesty, it was a miracle I'd even recognized *Daniel* that first time.

When Carol stayed quiet my gaze wandered to Beth who also stayed quiet. I hated the thought of her hurting from her ex's death. She still cared for him and her sister, even if she had been done so wrong by them. They were her family for such a long time. Sometimes it was hard to shut your heart off from something like that.

In fact, Deva and I were the only ones out of our group that seemed to be moving on. Maybe we were the only ones that were ready to? I did hope that Beth would get there eventually. All of my friends deserved to be happy, but Beth deserved to have someone love her for exactly who she is, just like Deva deserved to be appreciated for her amazing talents.

Carol seemed happy enough on her own, but I'd catch her looking distant sometimes, and not that creative distance where I could see that she was working on something either. This was a lonely distance. One that only came from being by yourself for a long time. One that I recognized all too well, though I would have denied it at the time as well.

Are we going to talk all day or hunt some toads? Buster asked, startling me out of my deep thoughts.

"Is Mr. Grumpy ready already?" I asked as he jumped up onto the table and sat in front of a plate of eggs that Deva had made just for him. He may have been a cat, but he was a cat with taste, and if we needed him then the last thing I wanted was for him to be grumpy and dragging his feet.

He sucked in a deep breath. *You spiced it with catnip, you wonderful chef, you.*

Well, that would perk him right up, I hoped. Couldn't catnip make some cats pass out as well? I hoped Buster was more a peppy nipper than a sleepy nipper because I had a feeling we were going to need his help today.

SIX

Daniel

"Geez, guys, I really appreciate you coming." I rubbed the back of my neck and smiled at Emma's brother and his girlfriend. I hoped Henry didn't think I was taking advantage of my friendship with his sister. He was a good guy, and I really did appreciate him helping me. He was still very much in his thirties, and probably still felt like he was in his twenties, even I felt that way sometimes, until I did something extravagant like tie my shoes and my back protested. He and Alice were a good fit, that much was obvious from just looking at them together.

Henry nodded his head once, quiet as he normally was around me. For the first time I realized that he had the same deep chestnut eyes as Emma. There was no doubt that they were brother and sister once you saw it. Out of the corner of my eye I saw Alice cock her head at me and stare steadily as she asked, "What's this all about?"

I shifted from one foot to the other. Yes, I lived in a town full of supernatural beings, but that didn't mean that it was an anything goes type of situation. Besides, Henry was human, yes, a human that knew about the truth of things, but still human, nonetheless. And Alice? Well, I wasn't really sure where she fell on the spectrum, but from what Emma had said she was some kind of witch or maybe she was just sensitive. It was hard to say.

After a moment I took a deep breath and as matter-of-factly as I could I said, "I feel kind of crazy about it, is the thing. But my best friend, he died years and years ago. And yesterday, he appeared to me. Here." I motioned toward the rock. "As a ghost."

That got Henry's attention and his dark eyes widened. "Like, white and filmy? As in Casper, the friendly?"

I nodded. "Yes. But he couldn't speak to me. He was trying to, but nothing came out, or through or whatever."

"So, why us?" Alice asked with her head still cocked. She reminded me a little of a dog that had heard a strange noise. No, scratch that, she reminded me of a bird that was curious about something.

I got the feeling she was evaluating me, deciding how honest to be, how much effort to put into helping me, that kind of thing, which I completely understood. Sometimes you could move heaven and earth to help someone, and they'd think it was nothing, the same as grabbing someone a drink while you were already in the kitchen, that type of thing. Then there were other people who would fight you when you tried to help them. While I was a cop, I'd seen it all, so I understood where Alice was coming from.

Honesty is always the best approach in my book, except when it comes to keeping the supernatural secret of course, so I said, "Well, I'm friends with Emma. And I know about her particular abilities."

"And she's told you about mine?" Alice guessed, which made Henry scowl.

I grinned apologetically. "Yes, but please don't think we were gossiping or anything like that. She's new to this world and I'm a shifter. So, I sort of already could tell you had extra abilities, but I wasn't sure what they were."

She accepted that explanation with a nod of her head. "All right, then. Tell me more about your friend."

"Thomas, as I said, was my best friend. We were more like brothers really. As a bear, I don't have a pack to speak of. But when he became alpha, the wolves welcomed me in as one of their own. I'm still connected to the pack, but not like I was when he was alive."

"You don't have your own family?" Henry asked, blunt as ever.

I sucked in a deep breath, still rattled by seeing Thomas yesterday and now by Henry's somewhat unexpected question. I tried to be as clinical about it as possible. Bears weren't known for being emotional, except when we were angry, but that didn't mean that we didn't feel things just as deeply as anyone else. In fact, sometimes I wondered if we actually felt things deeper, we just kept it to ourselves. "I had a family, unfortunately they all died and then my wife was in the same accident as Thomas." I sighed, trying to alleviate some of the pain in my chest before I continued. "I've failed his son. The pack is aimless, wild. Nathan has lost his way, and I should've helped him." It was hard to meet her gaze, or Henry's quiet one. "I've failed Thomas."

"Okay," Alice said in a soft voice. "I'll help you."

She walked over to the rock and climbed carefully up. Her t-shirt was plastered with animal cartoons on the back and said something about a 5k run for a local shelter and it was tucked into her jeans which in turn were tucked into her hiking boots. At least she'd come prepared for the terrain.

Her hair was pulled back in a tight bun, the auburn locks shining in the sun, looking redder than the normal brown. She had a natural, no-makeup-required beauty which matched her no-nonsense attitude. Henry held out a hand to help her step over the rough surface. She went to the area where Thomas had appeared. I wondered if it was something she could instinctively feel. I didn't know. Honestly, I had no idea how her gifts worked.

I opened my mouth to ask what she was doing, but she turned her head sharply to look at me squinting her dark eyes as she said, "Shh."

Okay, then. I stepped back and clamped my lips shut, shoving my hands in my pockets so I didn't fidget too much, and just watched.

Once Henry had Alice settled on the rock, he walked away and stood beside me. "Isn't she amazing?" he asked quietly. He wasn't a particularly emotive person, but even I could see the love shining in his eyes. I wondered if they'd said the L-word yet? If not, then they were fooling themselves that that wasn't what this was.

I wasn't sure what to call Alice's skills since she just sat there, legs crossed, eyes closed... not really doing anything. But these things weren't always visible, like Emma's powers, so for all I knew she was communing with all the dead spirits in the land.

That was probably a long list. This could take a while.

Henry and I backed away and found a moss-covered log to sit on, not too far away. After a few minutes, Henry pulled a bag out of the small pouch around his waist. I'd been wondering what he had in there.

"Cucumber?" he asked and held out the bag. It held slices of cucumber.

Well, I didn't want to be rude. "Thanks."

What an odd snack to have in his fanny pack. Was it just filled with snacks? That didn't seem quite like him though, I figured there'd be bandages and anti-itch creams or something as well, just in case. I knew Henry liked to be prepared.

As if he'd seen me staring curiously at the cucumber slice between my fingers, he explained. "They're full of water. As long as you keep them from getting crushed, they're a nice snack on a hike." He held the baggie out in my direction once more.

I grunted and took another. "Good idea."

If they hadn't been warm, they would've actually been refreshing.

By the time Alice opened her eyes, we'd gone through Henry's cucumbers and a small bag of chocolate chips. Who just carried around chocolate chips? Also, they were starting to melt.

"Are chocolate chips good for something on a hike?" I asked as I took a small handful. I had to lick my fingers after popping them in my mouth because of the sticky chocolate.

He shrugged. "I just like them."

"Okay," Alice said as she relaxed and shook out her hands. From the way she was moving it looked like she'd been tense the entire time she was doing...whatever it was she was doing.

Henry rushed forward when Alice lurched to the side. She was still sitting on the rock, but if she'd been standing, she might've actually fallen over. My stomach turned at the thought. "Alice," he cried as he reached her. "Are you okay?"

"Yeah." She cleared her throat and fixed her gaze on me as I walked toward them. "There was a spirit here. An air of..." She sucked in a deep breath. "Worry." But then she shook her head. "No. More than worry. The spirit was concerned enough to try to cross over. To warn someone. Whatever the warning is, you should take it seriously." She focused on me, furrowing her brow. "Very seriously." She reminded me of an angry schoolteacher.

I nodded. I'd suspected something like that. "Is there any way to know what he was trying to warn me about?"

She shook her head. "No. Unless he tries to cross over again, there's no way. Or if someone powerful can pull him back."

"Can I try to get to him?" I asked.

Again, she shook her head. "I tried. He's gone at peace. He only broke his rest to warn you. And I'm not strong enough to overpower him at his rest."

"Thank you." I shook both of their hands and they smiled and nodded at me. I thanked them again just to be sure that they understood how appreciative I was, especially after Alice had nearly fallen. "Do you want me to walk you down the trail?"

Henry shook his head and showed me a second, bigger pack on his side I hadn't noticed before. "We're going to keep hiking a while. I've got more snacks."

I chuckled. "Okay. If you ever need a favor in return, you know where to find me."

After they headed higher up into the mountains, I made my way back down the trail to my truck and headed for town. I had a lot to think about, trying to figure out what Thomas had wanted me to know.

As I traveled down the winding mountain road, a car veered over into my lane. It wasn't a big lane to begin with so sometimes things like that happened, especially if the other driver was unfamiliar with the area. I had to swerve to avoid it though.

I tried to correct my swerve, but my tires were too far over the line, and I was fighting to stay on the road. My heart pounded in my chest as I struggled with the truck. I couldn't keep it where it needed to be though, not without losing a wheel or something. The whole thing ended up rolling off the embankment. I was able to correct at the last moment, so I was basically just off roading down the side of the mountain - that was covered in trees.

All I had to do was not hit one.

SEVEN

Emma

We all held our breath when we opened the door and Buster stepped out. There was a part of me that just kept thinking back to the creepy letters I'd been receiving in Mystic Hollow. Someone knew what I'd done to my ex and his mistress. And if I couldn't get this right, I knew trouble was headed for me.

Whether it was because that creepy person would hurt me, some supernatural police were going to come for me, or if the actual human police would find enough to throw me in the slammer, I didn't know. Either way, I really needed to find them. I just hoped Buster was as good at tracking as Beth had claimed he was.

"Anything?" I asked, as Buster slowly inched toward my backyard.

Patience, human. Buster's voice sounded in my head. Beth had worked some magic when we came out so that Buster could talk to us without anyone else seeing it. The last thing we needed was the neighbors calling the police.

Beth touched my shoulder and shook her head.

Okay, I could be quiet. I was a quiet person. I didn't need to babble and fill the space with noise just because I felt like I was losing my head, maybe had a crazy stalker, and most definitely was on the radar of the police. Yeah, I could be—

They were here. Their magical scent is all over the place. Buster shook his head and sneezed. *It's overpowering.*

"Can you track it?" Beth asked.

Buster sniffed and gave her a haughty look. *Of course. I'm the best.*

"He really is," Beth said, giving him a smile. "He's a better tracker than lions and bears."

Those giant jerks are nothing compared to me. Buster said, with a haughty swish of his tail.

Beth looked at us and winked.

Buster started sniffing around the garden, starting at the door, and moving through the array of beautiful plants.

I couldn't help myself. I took a deep breath. A light breeze moved through the different plants and flowers, and the big trees gave the whole place some shade. In the background, I could still hear my little fountain by the pond going. The garden didn't feel like the house did. It felt like something that belonged to me and me alone. Rick had never cared so long as the front yard was green and mowed, I could do whatever I wanted back there.

I'd long ago turned our backyard into an oasis. It was the place that I let all the creative energy I couldn't use while spending the majority of my time on Rick's business. When Travis was younger, that extra energy had gone to him. But since he'd needed me less, this garden had become a special place just for me.

Rick had hated being back there, so I'd made it my own. A little pond, beautiful flowers everywhere. The scent of lavender wafting from the flowers I let grow wild and the splash of the fish in the pond. Yes, some of my plants were looking worse for the wear since I'd been gone, and weeds had definitely sprung up all over the place, but Travis had been kind enough to try to keep it all in decent shape when he could get away from classes.

Man, I didn't know what I'd done to deserve that kid.

But overall, as I watched Buster try to pick his way through the chaos, my gaze picked out more and more changes since I'd been here last. Everything needed pruning and the patches of grass, which I normally kept trimmed and neat, were wild. No doubt the yard was full of mice and snakes.

And hopefully, frogs. Or, rather, toads.

This way, Buster said. He had his nose to the ground and his tail swished back and forth as he weaved to and fro through the flowers and shrubs. *Nope,* he eventually said, sitting back on his haunches. *Not here.*

"Where then?" I asked.

Buster looked out the gate. *That way.*

They were somewhere in the neighborhood? Maybe further?

I sighed. "I was afraid of that. They could've gotten anywhere in the weeks I've been gone."

With a big inhale, our feline helper shook his head. *No, the smell is too fresh. They've been keeping to this area, and they're together.*

Well, that was promising. "Lead on, but you need to act like a real cat," I said.

He rolled his eyes—first time I'd ever seen a cat roll his eyes—and trotted forward. *This isn't my first search and rescue. And I am a real cat.*

How many frogs had this cat found? Surely this wasn't a normal occurrence.

"Hello!"

"Oh, no," I muttered. I'd know that shrill voice anywhere. Plastering a big, fake smile on my face, I turned to the right to face my oldest, busybodiest neighbor. Mrs. Brennan. "Hello, Mrs. B. How are you?"

"Well, it's nice to see you home. I hope you plan to take care of your yard soon." She patted her short, blonde hair as if she was some housewife from the fifties, then ran her hands down the apron, covered in pictures of apples, as if it were wrinkled.

It wasn't wrinkled. She knew it wasn't wrinkled. Her clothes were *never* wrinkled. I couldn't ever figure out if it was a nervous habit, or a way of her reminding me that I had plenty of wrinkles in sight. But as her judgy gaze swept over my much rounder body, and her nose wrinkled, I suspected the latter.

Man, we'd barely been back here, and I was itching to turn this woman into a toad too. I needed therapy, and lots of it.

Gritting my teeth, I stared at the tiny woman. "I'll get right on that. Wouldn't want to bother you with a messy yard."

She sniffed. "It's all right, dear. I didn't understand why your son couldn't have done a better job with it. But maybe he takes after your husband."

Her words dropped between us like stones.

She looked disappointed when I didn't react. "Didn't he leave you for a younger woman?"

"Yeah?" I said with an edge in my voice. She was always hateful and nosy, but this was pushing dangerous territory.

"So, it makes sense your son might be done wasting his time around here too."

I curled my hands into fists. *Do not turn her into a toad. No matter how funny it would be to see a skinny toad with warts wearing her apron.* My magic had already gotten me into enough trouble.

After pushing her glasses up on her nose and clearing her throat, Mrs. Brennan just couldn't seem to stop herself. "Perhaps your husband would've been here if you'd taken my advice before. Had dinner ready for him, fixed your face." She softened her expression as I glared, as if she cared about me enough to give me this sage wisdom.

"*Hey,*" Deva said loudly.

Carol stepped forward. "Rick was a loser. He didn't deserve a minute with Emma, much less the years she gave him. Not that it's *any* of your business."

Beth tossed her long, blonde hair back. "What's happened in your life to make you so miserable that you'd talk to someone like that?"

"My guess is that all she has to offer any man are *meals,*" Deva glared.

"At least my man comes home every evening," Mrs. B gave me a dirty look. "I'd hate to be old *and* single."

"Who you calling old?" Deva challenged.

Mrs. B nodded toward me. "She ruined her looks with work, when she should have been moisturizing, cooking, and cleaning."

Beth started taking out her earrings. "Those are fighting words, Miss Skinny Bitch."

Uh oh.

I held up a hand. "It's okay." But even as I said the words, my magic had begun to tingle. Taking my arms, I spread them toward Mrs. Brennan's perfectly manicured garden, hoping to lessen whatever Karma had in store this time. And in an instant, I realized Karma had created the perfect revenge. "Geez, Mrs. B. Looks like you've got some weeds in your garden."

She turned slowly around, with her nose wrinkled, and peered across the road toward her yard.

"Is that..." I gasped dramatically. "Is that a dandelion?" I tutted my tongue. "Once you get dandelions, you've got them for *life*."

My friends giggled with my emphasis on the word life. They knew what that meant. My magic would make sure old Mrs. B's yard would forever be plagued by the little poufy weeds.

"No. No, that's not..." She just continued staring in disbelief.

"And as for me, don't you worry your pretty little head. I'm enjoying life in my beach house, with my best friends, and the sexiest man alive. But you enjoy your... lawn and cooking."

"But I don't have weeds," she finally managed.

"You do now! Well, we'll leave you to your new wild-flowers," I chirped. "Ta!"

Giggling, we turned and followed Buster as he trotted up the sidewalk. To his credit, Buster was trying to act like a normal cat, but his nose kept sniffing around, and he kept looking back at us to make sure we were following him. Oh well, if anyone noticed his odd behavior, they wouldn't say anything. It'd just make them sound crazy.

Suddenly, the tabby froze and sniffed a lot in one spot. *I got something. This way,* Buster said and darted off the cement.

We hurried after him as he entered a small, wooded copse behind one of the houses up the street. "Wait," I called, trying to mask the fact that I was panting a little from hurrying after the darn cat. I didn't want my friends to think this little trek was enough to make me winded.

Luckily, it didn't take long to reach our destination. We hurried out of the trees and had to stop short to keep from running headlong into a large pond.

There you go, Buster said, sounding pleased with himself.

My jaw dropped. I'd walked by this pond before. It had never stood out to me as being anything other than a green, gross mess of water. But on an adventure to find two toads, the pond completely changed in front of me. As I eyed every water lily, plant, rock, and muddy area of shallow water I saw it. Toads. Frogs.

Everywhere.

"Oh, my goodness." I looked around, feeling my stomach flip. "How are we going to figure out which toads they are?"

Deva looked at Buster.

The cat stretched, circled, and settled onto the ground. *I've done my part. They're here. Most definitely.*

"Helpful," Deva mumbled.

And I swear, Buster gave her a dirty look.

Beth put her hands out. "I'm going to stretch my powers out and hear what they're thinking that should help!"

Flies.

My lily pad.

Nice, warm mud.

A thousand voices seemed to come at us at once. It was so overwhelming that I actually put my hands to my ears. Not that it helped. Their words were in my head.

"Okay, I'll ease back a little, so it isn't so much," Beth whispered, and then the voices got fewer and quieter.

I let out a breath and dropped my hands.

Flies, flies, flies.

Hungry.

My pond.

The voices were there still. Too many of them. Breaking into my mind like unwanted thoughts, but they were at least bearable. Throaty, more animalistic than any of the domesticated animals Beth cared for, but still there.

"Should be easy," Deva said. She put her hands around her mouth to amplify her voice. "Would the toad that happens to also be a dirty, cheating bastard please hop forward? Also, the cheap floozy he cheated with. If you'd like to be human again, I suggest you show yourselves."

Flies, flies.

Eat.

Food.

Human? Was human?

Cheat?

A couple of the voices separated themselves. Still throaty and animalistic, but with a touch of something almost human. My gut churned, and I waited. Whatever I'd done to them, would they have enough human left in them to actually step forward?

To my astonishment, two frogs or toads or whatever, hopped quickly toward us.

Me. Human. The voice held a note of my husband's.

Not floozy. Said a voice, with a feminine touch.

Beth pulled a small bag out of her pocket. "Hop in, jerks. And we'll get you back to normal."

Astonished, I laughed as they did as she asked. I should've been feeling guilty for putting them in this predicament to begin with, but somehow... I didn't.

Oh, well.

EIGHT

Emma

My nerves were shot by the time we got home. The toads had been muttering all sorts of weird things until Beth used her magic to turn their words back into ribbits, but even that hadn't soothed my nerves. Carol upended the bag and dumped the toads onto the middle of the kitchen floor, while Buster went to take, what he described as, *the much-needed nap of a hero.*

And then, it was just us and the toads. It was strange to see them. Two toads in the middle of the floor, on the tile that I'd picked out that looked like wood. In a kitchen that I'd put so many little touches on over years. Heck, I still had pictures of Travis and his various school pictures over the years hanging up. And for some reason, as my gaze roamed over the images of my son growing up, looking at his smile full of braces made this all feel real in a way it hadn't.

I'd turned my ex into a toad.

My husband of so many years had betrayed me, had cheated on me, and made me feel like I wasn't worthy of love. All of that had happened. All of it was part of the fabric of who I am now. Including these two toads. It felt like they were a representation of all the pain I'd felt when he'd cheat on me. Every time he had to "work late" and told me that I had been working so hard for so long, he wanted to help more, I dismissed the gut feeling that told me he would never do more work than he had to. I dismissed the gut feeling I had that him working late didn't seem to be lessening my workload. That voice in the back of my head was just too scary to listen to. I'd convinced myself that he was finally stepping up. That maybe, just maybe, things would actually get better for us in our golden years.

And then I found out he'd been banging his secretary, a girl I had helped mentor when he'd claimed to be working. I'd found out he'd taken her to *our* restaurant. And that the reason all our joint friends were suddenly too busy to hang out was because he'd introduced her to them...

I hadn't just been angry. I'd been hurt. Deeply hurt.

How was it that I moved from hurt to angry so fast and never actually stepped back to give myself a break and say it was okay to be hurt? I deserved to be upset. Just because Rick was a bad guy didn't mean I was somehow to blame for what happened to me.

I let out a slow breath, and it felt like so much of that hurt left in that breath. Maybe there would always be a tiny part of my heart that thought of the man I fell in love with and wished for that innocent love again. But most of me? Most of me was really ready to be done with this. I was ready to move on in my life, but also to move on from the ghosts of my past.

Starting with these two.

"You okay?" Beth asked.

I forced a smile but felt my eyes burning. "I'm okay."

She squeezed my shoulder. "When everything

happened with my ex, your calls got me through some of the darkest times. Watching him and my sister all throughout town, not even bothering to hide their relationship, it hurt. A lot. If I could've turned them into toads, I think I would have."

I laughed. "You're too nice for that."

Beth lifted a brow. "I was a doormat for a long time. I know you weren't around to see everything, but I'm not anymore. It took some therapy and some time to learn the difference between being nice and being a doormat, but now I know. And I don't let people push me around like that anymore."

I was surprised. I never knew Beth had gone through therapy. "You never said..."

She shrugged. "Sometimes people treat therapy like it's something to be ashamed of. And maybe, at first, I was. But we go to a doctor when we have a broken leg, why shouldn't we go to therapy when we have a broken heart?"

Damn. She was absolutely right.

"I went too," Deva said, squaring her shoulders.

I honestly felt shocked. Deva seemed like the kind of person who never needed anyone else to help her through hard times. She just took everything in strides.

She laughed. "It's true. I ended things with Harry because he made me feel like I didn't matter. Like I didn't exist. I'd try to look prettier, or cook more, or clean more. I'd go online and find clever stories to share with him. But no matter what I did, it wasn't enough. So, I saw a therapist. And I realized... well, he was a jerk. But that wasn't enough for me. I didn't want to just realize it wasn't all my fault, I wanted to not make the same mistake again. You guys have been encouraging me to date Marquis, but I honestly didn't feel ready until now. I wanted to make sure that if I started dating someone again, I wouldn't fall into the same pattern, or pick the same type of loser who doesn't know what he has until it's gone."

"Maybe I should've gone to therapy," Carol said softly.

We all turned and looked at her, waiting. Carol was always so calm and cheerful. She never seemed to want to share anything too deep. She'd smile and knit, and then surprise us with something we never even realized. But she couldn't be rushed, and we all knew it.

She began to pick at the rainbow-colored butterflies she'd sewn all over her bright yellow pants. "I felt like Bryan was the one. Deep in my heart. And maybe a therapist could've helped me realize that if he was the one, he wouldn't have just abandoned me and left without a word. Maybe I could've found someone else."

"Do you want someone else?" Deva asked quietly.

Carol was silent for a painfully long moment. "No, but I also think it's crazy that I've been pining for him all these years."

"That doesn't make you crazy," I said.

Her misty blue eyes met mine hesitantly. "Are you sure? Because most people would think I was crazy."

I reached out and squeezed her hand. "If you're crazy, we all are."

And then we were all laughing.

"We're quite a group," Deva said, running her hands over her short, dark hair in a nervous gesture.

"And I wouldn't have it any other way," I said, giving her my best reassuring look.

Everyone smiled.

And then, one of the toads made a terrible sound, and we all looked down. Oh yeah, there was still that to deal with. And yet, I didn't feel any anger when I looked at them now. I just felt a deep need to move on. They were my past, not my future.

"Well, now what?" Deva asked. "You know, you *could* leave them like that. Or put them in a terrarium and every time you think about how he hurt you, look at your pet toads. "

The idea didn't sound horrible, but I chuckled. "No, I've realized I've lost most of my anger. I just want to put him behind me and start my new life in Mystic Hollow."

Beth put her arm around my shoulders. "That sounds like you're processing your emotions well. We're so proud of you."

I chuckled and stared down at the handiwork of my volatile magic. Yeah, *now* I was processing my emotions in a healthy way. And yet, even though I had much better control over my magic, I still had no idea how to change them back. "But how do I fix this?" I asked. "Now that I don't care what sort of lesson they do or don't learn, and I'm ready to turn them back into humans, how does Karma... let go of a grudge?"

"Maybe just concentrate on them and that feeling?" Carol suggested.

I focused on them, trying to lasso my power and send it toward the toads sitting on the kitchen floor, but nothing happened. A headache began in the middle of my forehead. But I kept focusing, and still, nothing happened.

"Maybe we can help," Beth said. "Just think that Karma has been appeased and we'll lend you our power, too."

"Okay," I whispered and focused again as my friends put their hands on my back. It was strange how I felt their magic wash over me. It was almost like feeling the love from a friend through the phone. It made every hair on my body stand on end, and I swore I could sense each of them separately.

Beth's magic was like her. She was short in stature, but never in heart. I pictured her taking out her earrings, ready to fight my neighbor. Her magic felt like that, like something small but powerful. I sensed her connection to the world too. It was like a pink web spreading out to all the other life and connecting her in a way that was beautiful.

Deva's magic came with a scent like the most delicious cookies in the world. I could practically see her. A strong black woman who ventured out and started her own business. She'd worked day and night, and her magic weaved through every piece of food she made. And yet, it was more than that. Her food touched people. It became a part of them. It soothed them when they were struggling, made them laugh, and even cry.

Carol's magic was beautiful. A rainbow of colors like her knitting. But not *just* like her knitting, like her outfits, which were always wild and creative. Like her hair, that always had a certain lovable messiness. Like her spirit. If she were an animal, I got the craziest feeling she'd be a Pegasus. That she'd be like the sun and the moon and the wind, altogether.

"Focus, Emma," Beth whispered.

I felt tears blur my eyes. "You're all just so beautiful. You, your magic, it's beautiful, just like you."

"You can compliment us later," Deva said, laughter in her voice. "Fix the toads."

Right, focus! I pulled my focus from the magic to the two toads, and then felt my friends' magic weaving with my own. It felt right...stronger.

"They don't need me to punish them," I muttered as I focused. *And this isn't justice, or karmic justice any longer.*

I felt it. My magic moving, flowing, shaping. There was a moment I wasn't sure what it would do. Like, me and my karmic powers were two separate things, and I had no real control over it. And then I knew, the magic had made its decision.

Whatever was meant to happen, would happen.

And just like that, the magic relented. Rick and Candy appeared in front of me with a pop, naked and disheveled.

They looked at each other, then at us in shock.

"What are you doing here, naked?" Deva asked, sounding outraged. She turned to me. "I'm so sorry. They've obviously taken drugs or something."

There was a tense moment when I wasn't sure if they'd buy it, and then Candace glared at my ex. "What the hell?" Candace said. "Where did you get those mushrooms?"

She stared at Rick and then belatedly seemed to remember us standing there. "Oh!" Looking down, she suddenly saw that she wore no clothes and squeaked before running out of the room. Rick followed behind, but not before shooting me a suspicious look.

"They think they've been high all this time," Deva whispered. "That couldn't have worked out better."

"You're a genius," Carol said with a laugh as she bumped Deva's shoulder with her own.

But I didn't feel much better. The whole thing left me feeling a little defeated. What good had all of it been? I walked out to my garden while the girls chattered and started lunch. It also made me sad to see it in this state, not that I'd ever admit that to the nosy neighbor. But this had been my happy place, out here in the greenery, and it was gone to pot now.

"Emma?"

I stiffened when I heard Rick's voice. "What?" I asked. "Do we have to get into it right now?"

He circled the bench I sat on and stood in front of me. "Actually, I wanted to tell you that you deserved better than me."

My jaw unhinged. I never in a million years would've expected to hear that come out of his mouth. "What?"

"I'm going to sell the house and I'll give you the value of half the business and half the house's selling price," he said. "You deserve more, but that's the best I can do."

"Thanks," I said.

He ran his hand through his balding hair. "I don't know what came over me. I guess I just got so used to you giving and giving, and me taking and taking, that it felt right at the time. It was like all that mattered was what I wanted. But something... I don't know... made me realize that I'm just a small part of a bigger world, and that nothing does, or should, revolve around me."

So, his time as a toad had done him some good after all. I cocked my head. "I'm moving back home to be near Henry."

Rick looked surprised, and then he gave a tentative smile. "You also talked about that place like it was perfect."

"It is," I told him.

He nodded. "And I understand you wanting to get out of town. What was the name of your hometown?"

I almost didn't tell him, for fear he'd look me up, but that seemed unlikely. "Mystic Hollow."

Rick stiffened. "What?"

I raised my eyebrows. "What, what?"

Seriously, it took effort not to get mad. I talked about my hometown a lot. The fact that he didn't know after all this time was yet another reason he was an ass. I was half tempted to look away from him and ask him what color my eyes were. But I don't think I needed more proof that he hadn't cared one bit about me.

"It's nothing..." he said.

"It doesn't sound like nothing," I said, feeling more and more uncomfortable by the second.

He seemed to realize I was getting freaked out and gentled his voice. "I didn't realize you were from Mystic Hollow. That's such an odd coincidence. A friend of mine, sort of. A guy I know, Al, works remotely for a company we do a lot of work with. We've become sort of friends over the last ten years."

The hairs on the back of my neck stood on end. How in the world did Rick know Al from Mystic Hollow? And what did that mean for us? Who the hell was Al? Maybe Daniel knew him.

"No one has said anything to me about knowing you," I told him.

He winced. "Well, I haven't exactly told him flattering stories about you..."

I stood, needing to get out of there. Because if I didn't, I was either going to start obsessing about what this all meant or turn Rick into a toad again.

"Thanks for being fair about the divorce."

"It's the least I could do."

Yeah, Rick, yeah it is.

NINE

Daniel

"What a pain in the ass," I muttered as I shook Sheriff Danvers's hand. The tow truck had just left with my own truck, the chains hooked under the front bumper and the whole thing secured so it just coasted on the back wheels. At least I wasn't hurt. Perk of being a shifter. I would've been pretty damn banged and bruised up if I'd been human, but I was already fine. I wasn't sure my truck would be salvageable, but at least I was.

"Come on," Danvers said. "I'll give you a lift to the mechanic."

I gave him all the information I had, which wasn't much. I'd barely seen the car, other than it being small and silver. There weren't any tracks on the ground and by the time I'd stopped somewhat safely in the huge ditch, nearly a ravine, their scent had faded.

Danvers dropped me off at the mechanic right behind my truck. I'd called on the way and my buddy who owned the shop, Joel, was going to let me borrow one of his old trucks while he fixed mine. And he did mean old.

It was a brown that could only have been found in the fifties or sixties with a thick cream stripe down the sides that had probably been white at one point. Instead of sitting high like most pickups these days did, this thing was almost a low rider. The bench seat was covered in what was essentially corduroy and while there was a seatbelt it looked like it had been a later addition to the truck. The bed swooped out from the cab and looked more like an afterthought than something that was designed to be functional.

Danvers leaned against the driver's side window of my loaner and rubbed his eyes in a way I recognized all too well. It was the exhaustion of being constantly worried, the weight of being sheriff that rested across his shoulders and his mind at night, making sleep difficult to find and maintain. I adjusted the mirrors and everything so I could actually see and drive safely. Sure, I have shifter reflexes, but even those aren't enough once you're going fast enough, and I wasn't about to have any other lives on my conscience. "This town has had some bad luck with car accidents, and I'm about sick of working them. You're damn lucky you didn't hit one of those trees before you were able to slow down, or this would've been a very different day."

Joel nodded and they kept discussing the wrecks, but I sort of tuned them out. I could feel myself mechanically nodding along at the right times. The truth was the last thing I wanted to think about was when my wife and best friend died. Or Emma's parents for that matter. There were more than that, but those were the ones I'd personally known. Joel and Danvers were right though, our town had more than its fair share of accidents, and in turn deaths. I never understood why. The only thing people ever seemed to blame was the mountain roads.

"A real tragedy, what happened to Thomas and Sarah," Joel muttered.

Thomas and Sarah's names caught my ear. Joel had known my wife as well, so he knew how much car accidents hit home for me. "We should grab a beer together sometime." It would be nice to start actually connecting with people again and stop punishing myself for their deaths. I wasn't guilty of anything, I couldn't even claim survivors' guilt, and yet that's what it felt like, like I should have died in that accident with them.

Joel grinned at me, blue eyes sparkling with mischief. "You buyin'?"

I snorted and smiled back, forcing my face to do what I needed it to even if my brain didn't feel like it after everything that had happened and thinking about all the deaths that had touched my life. "Why not?" I could do this whole friendship thing. It wasn't a completely foreign concept to me, just a muscle I hadn't really stretched in a long time.

I circled the truck so I could head out going the right direction, when Danvers shouted, "Hey, hang on, fellas." I braked and put it back in park. "What's up?" I asked leaning out of the open window to look behind me as I tried to follow Danvers' gaze.

"Something's leaking."

That was all I needed to hear to have me turning the truck off and getting out. Whatever it was had to have just happened. If I knew one thing it was that Joel wouldn't put me in a faulty truck.

Joel bent over and swiped his finger through the liquid dripping from behind the truck's tire. "That's brake fluid," he said. "Shit, Danny, I'm sorry. Here we were talking about wrecks, and I would've sent you out in a truck that would've caused one."

I backed up, so Joel didn't think I was crowding him, and shook my head. "It's like fate is out to get me."

Damn. Had I done something to piss Emma off? I wracked my brain but couldn't think of anything that would get her upset enough to set her magic on me. Maybe it was one of the witches? I'd certainly seen some strange things lately, and that's saying something.

"Come on," Danvers said. "I'll drive the squad car home tonight. You can borrow my truck for a few days while Joel here tries his best to bring yours back to life."

They slapped each other on the back and teased a little bit more, then I got back in the squad car we'd pulled up in. Danvers got in next to me and rolled down his window, waving goodbye to Joel as we pulled out of the lot and headed toward the center of town where the station and Danvers' truck were. I would have offered to take the squad car, but even though I'd been on the force for a while I doubted they'd be comfortable letting me use something like that.

"Is there anyone at all who could have a beef with you?" Danvers asked for the third time once we were back on the road. "What about the alpha?"

I shook my head. "I'm not saying it's impossible, but I don't think so. The kid wouldn't react like that." I couldn't believe it was Nathan, even if I had shown him a little tough love, it wasn't like the kid was vindictive, plus I didn't think he'd know his brake line from his transmission.

Danvers grunted. He wasn't so convinced. We pulled into the police station just down the road and I got his keys. "Thanks, man. I really appreciate it and I'll try my best not to let anyone run me off the road in this one."

The joke fell a little flat. We both knew that if someone

wanted me dead, they wouldn't be waiting until I had my own truck again.

As I pulled out in my friend's truck, heading toward home, I thought about the warning Thomas had been trying to give me. Whatever the reasoning behind this incident, one thing I knew for sure was it was no accident. Someone wanted me dead, and I had two problems I needed to figure out to stop them, who they were, and why they wanted me off the mortal coil. The biggest problem was the fact that I had no idea where to start.

TEN

Emma

Ahh, it was nice to be home. Even though home was just a bedroom to myself in my parents' house, which now belonged to Henry and me. It still felt amazing to be here. There was something inherently relaxing about my parents' place. I couldn't say it was that I'd always felt safe here, though I had...It was something else, something that made me wonder if all the love that we felt for each other as a family had seeped into the walls, just like all the sadness I'd felt in my marriage had soaked into the old house.

It had taken three weeks to get everything taken care of. The house sold the day we put it on the market. The agent had expected it. I'd priced it to move, as well. And Rick had been cooperative, so everything lined up. I just hoped that the heavy feeling that Carol and the other ladies could sense didn't get transferred to the new owners somehow.

I'd used a moving company and separated out my things from his, sent his stuff to him and mine here. I still hadn't unpacked the first box, but the downstairs and my room was full of them, plus a storage unit Henry had rented for me.

I'd marked which boxes should come to the house and which needed to go to storage. All of Travis and Jacqueline's stuff had gone straight to storage since none of that was mine, and they said they'd take care of it when they got back. I'd donated a *lot* of stuff, too. That had felt good, knowing someone would get some good use out of things I no longer needed.

I looked over at the manila envelope on the nightstand. It was thicker than I'd expected, filled to the brim with my divorce papers, signed and ready to deliver to my lawyer tomorrow. I just didn't have the energy today after rolling into town. My girls had rented a car and gone back once we'd settled Rick. They hadn't been able to stay all three weeks with me. I'd missed them. More than ever before if I was honest.

Every time I'd left home before it was exciting, and I couldn't wait to get back to whatever it was I'd been doing before I left. Or I was stressed about all the work that needed to be done, which was honestly why my visits had become fewer and fewer. Over time it had become easier to FaceTime with Henry than come all the way out here. I think subconsciously I also remembered how happy and free I'd been here and that definitely hadn't been true of my married life, with the exception of Travis.

Henry had welcomed me back, though he had been on his way out to see Alice. The movers had dropped everything off the day before, so it was just me and my stuff now. With the house all to myself the only thing I wanted right now though was a nap. When I woke up, I'd make myself some dinner and have that and a glass of wine on the back deck as I listened to the waves crashing against the shore.

The evening sounded just about perfect or would have if I'd have someone to share it with. It wasn't that I couldn't be alone, but I enjoyed the company of others. I wasn't one of those people that could hole themselves up in their house and exist on take out and TV. Not that there's anything wrong with that, it just wasn't me.

I loved being around my friends, chatting and laughing as we told stories and had adventures. Having Travis had been an adventure unlike any other, and I wouldn't change it for the world, but I was grateful to be where I was, with the friends I had, and finally knowing the truth about the world.

As I closed my eyes, I thought about saying goodbye to Travis. He and Jacqueline were in Paris now, excited and having the time of their lives. I was so glad they'd gotten this opportunity. Travis sent me pictures all throughout the day yesterday and in the early hours of the morning of things they were seeing and experiencing. I knew it was the early hours of the morning not only because of the time stamp, but because I'd been too excited to be free of my life in Springfield and had been up early driving. The time difference between us was going to take some getting used to.

I was jealous in some ways, though incredibly grateful they'd had this opportunity. I should have taken the chance when I was in college, but I was too head over heels for Rick to want to be away from him for a whole semester.

In a way, Travis and I were both experiencing a new world. Here I was, finally, free. Free to be my own person, to grow and thrive without Rick hanging over me like a dark cloud.

The early afternoon sun was streaming in my window, and I could hear life passing by outside along with the ocean in the distance as sleep began to drift over me, and I felt more relaxed than I had in ages, at least until my phone dinged. I grabbed it, because it was the special tone I'd set for Daniel, and rolled onto my back, holding my phone over my face as I read what he had to say.

Would you like to go to dinner? I saw your car in the driveway as I passed by today. I'd love to sit down and talk.

Talk, huh? What did that mean? I chuckled as my fingers flew over the screen. **Oh, so now you're stalking me?**

His reply came quickly which made my heart do a little flip in my chest. The idea that he'd been waiting for my reply was sweet and not one I was going to dissuade myself of just yet. **No! Not at all.**

The dots that let me know he was typing appeared on the screen just under his text, so I waited. My nervous heart beating rapidly in my chest at what he might say. A second reply came a minute later. **I go past your house and cut through Harper St. to get to my house from town.**

Poor guy. He thought I was really upset. **I'm just messing with you. I'd love to have dinner. When?**

Tonight. I'll pick you up at 7pm. He replied quickly. He'd known I'd say yes, or at least suspected and had a plan. He wasn't asking where I wanted to go or being wishy-washy about things, and I appreciated that. Sometimes having someone just tell you the plan was all you needed. I trusted Daniel and I knew he wouldn't take me somewhere horrible.

It's a date.

I let my arm fall back on to the bed and couldn't stop the giddy feeling that was growing inside me. I left my phone on the bed as I jumped up, my previous exhaustion forgotten in the excitement of the date. I brushed out my hair and thought about Daniel in high school versus Daniel now. He'd always been hot, but now he was... well, he was a bear. And not just a shifter. But besides his looks, he was protective and caring. And smart... and funny.

Okay, maybe I liked him a little. I took my time getting ready and wondering what he would think of me now if he could see me back in high school. As I swiped on one more layer of mascara, I chuckled. Probably would've run screaming. That was a *very* long time ago.

A few hours later, the doorbell rang as I slipped on my sandals, so I turned and opened it.

He looked surprised, standing in front of me in a tee and jeans that had seen better days. "Oh, you look great."

I looked down at the dress I'd slipped on. "Well, I try not to look like a cave troll when I go on a date."

Daniel opened his mouth as though he was going to say something a few times and the realization that he hadn't seen this as a date sank in. "This is just two friends going to talk, isn't it?" I could hear the disappointment in my own voice, I just hoped he couldn't. I was freshly divorced, I probably wasn't even ready to date, yet... Daniel was, well, Daniel and I'd wanted this to be a date more than I'd thought.

With his eyes widening, Daniel held up his hands. "No, I'm perfectly happy to call this a date. I always want to go on a date with you, Emma."

A warm little flame flickered to life in my heart. Well, that made me feel good. I stepped out onto the porch. "Okay, then, it's a date." Why not?

As I turned to lock the door, my heart skipped a beat when I caught a flash of white out of the corner of my eye. It wasn't just any white though, it was a very specific white, one I'd only seen a couple times before. "What was that?" I breathed.

"What?" Daniel was instantly on alert as he looked around the front yard. "I don't see anything."

For a second, I would've sworn a ghost had stood on the side of the porch, but there wasn't anyone there now. It was probably just me being super tired. "Nothing. I'm being silly. Let's go." Maybe I was just remembering the last ghost I'd seen on the porch. That hadn't exactly been fun.

I could tell that Daniel wasn't entirely convinced, but we headed down the steps and along the path making out way to his truck anyway, though the alert posture he'd taken never really went away. "Did you paint your truck?" I asked. The rich hunter green was definitely not the same as the beat up dark blue it had been. There had been scratches along the sides where he'd obviously driven too close to the same trees over and over again that were gone now.

He grinned. "Different truck. This is a loaner until Joel can get to mine and bang out the damage from the wreck."

"Wait." I stopped and put my hand on his arm. His words were like a vice around my heart. "You were in a wreck?"

He chuckled and opened the passenger door. "Come on. I'll explain on the way." He may not have thought it was a big deal, but car accidents weren't exactly things that gave me the warm fuzzies. Not when that's how I'd lost my parents. The idea that I could have lost Daniel and not even known about it until I came back to town made my stomach twist. The supernatural world was dangerous, and I almost expected the people I cared about to be in danger because of it, but from a car accident? That kind of thing seemed unlikely now, even though I was apparently wrong.

ELEVEN

Emma

The restaurant Daniel had chosen was one I hadn't been to before. It was a small Italian food place with romantic music, big plates full of food, and lots of bricks showing on the walls. They'd also decorated with a lot of red and green, so the place officially felt like a little slice of Italy.

I felt oddly flattered. Living here all my life, I knew this was one of the fancy places. The fact that Daniel chose this place, even though it wasn't *officially* a date, made me feel like he was trying to impress me. I couldn't remember the last time a man tried to impress me.

The waitress gave us a sweet smile and set my lasagna in front of me, and his chicken parmesan. They'd already given us really soft bread and this green dipping sauce that tasted like heaven. I knew I shouldn't still be quite this hungry, but everything just tasted so darn good that I couldn't help myself.

Grabbing my fork like a child who'd just been given cake, I dug into my food. Instantly the cheesy goodness melted into my mouth, and I groaned. The sauce was just the perfect mix of sweet and savory. When I'd first seen the giant plate, I'd thought there was no chance I could finish it, but now I just couldn't seem to stop eating.

I'd need to tell the others about this place. Or not. Because I had a feeling we'd all end up here every day.

"I like a woman who eats," Daniel said.

Glancing up, I froze, every muscle in my body tense. But his eyes were filled with happiness, not judgment. This wasn't like when Rick would remind me that I need to watch my carbs. Daniel actually meant what he was saying.

My shoulders relaxed, and I snorted and rolled my eyes. "Next you'll be telling me to smile more."

He burst out laughing, a little loud, as if he were nervous about something. "No, I didn't mean it like that. Just, when I dated before, long ago..." He rolled his eyes. "Too long. It seemed like the women always pretended they didn't actually want to eat. It drove me crazy."

I nodded, understanding his intent. "Yeah, that was the thing to do in high school, so we could make sure we could fit into our acid wash jeans." I took another big bite of my lasagna and smiled inwardly at the memory of lying on my bed, sucking in my gut, and trying to get my tightest jeans to button.

Now, I only wore jeans on special occasions. Usually, I preferred leggings, jeggings, basically anything that was comfortable and didn't leave me with a muffin top.

"I wouldn't mind seeing you smile more, though," Daniel said. "And especially if I was the one who put the smile on your face."

I moaned around my next bite full of food and tried not to laugh. "Smooth." I rested my forehead on my hand and chuckled at that killer line.

He shook his head with a grin. "Sorry, I'm a little rusty."

"I'm rusty at everything," I said, then realized what I was implying and felt my cheeks burning.

He threw back his head and laughed out loud. And I swear, I'd never seen a guy look so handsome. His auburn hair, with the gray at his temples, brought out his sun kissed skin. And his green eyes were filled with a kind of joy that lit his entire handsome face up.

If I could have bottled up the sight of him and kept it forever, I would have. Even when his laugh died, and his gaze fell on me again, it felt like my heart was swelling.

Is this what a good date felt like? Or just sharing company with someone who was genuinely good? I had no idea. But it felt so dang right.

We went back to eating, not talking much. And to my surprise, the silence felt comfortable. Not the least bit strained. It was better than feeling like an old married couple. It was more like we just... fit together.

A few minutes later, he threw me another compliment. "Do you know you have beautiful hair?"

I patted the black mop on my head and grimaced. He really did like me if he thought my hair was beautiful. "I always wanted to cut it short, but Rick thought I'd look like a boy if I did."

Daniel's lips twitched at the mention of my ex-husband. "You'd look good even if you shaved it." He took a bite and chewed for a moment. "So, not to pry, but how'd the sale go?"

I grinned. "It went well. Took longer than I wanted to settle everything, but I'm officially divorced, and my house is sold. I'm a permanent resident of Mystic Hollow."

His big smile lit up the dimly lit restaurant. I wasn't the

only one who deserved compliments, but I didn't know exactly how to tell him.

"I'm really glad you're staying," he said in a quiet voice. "Maybe next time I can take you on a real date."

I shrugged. "I like Italian food, and the ambiance in here is great." Oh, yeah. This wasn't supposed to be a date. "For two friends, I mean," I said with one arched eyebrow. "So, why'd you want to *hang out* anyway?" I asked.

Daniel sucked in a deep breath as he wiped his mouth. "Well, it's a sensitive subject, I guess."

"I'm pretty sure everything I've discussed with you since coming here was a sensitive subject," I told him with a grin.

He lifted a brow. "You have a point there." He took a deep breath and all the joy faded from his face. "While you were gone, my best friend came to me."

That didn't seem all that strange, but he said the words like it was *very* significant. What was I missing here?

I nodded, trying not to give away my confusion. "Okay. What did he say?"

"No." Daniel shook his head, frowning. "I meant my best friend Thomas."

My fork clattered on my plate. His best friend, Thomas. The person who had died in a car accident with Daniel's wife. Beth had been the one to call and tell me about it, and it'd brought me painfully back to the day my parents had died. Since then, Daniel had spoken of it, but I'd tried really hard not to pry.

Still, I had a feeling if his best friend's ghost was regularly visiting him, this wouldn't be a big deal. What had gotten the bear shifter so upset?

"Oh," I murmured. "Okay."

Was this a good thing? I had no idea if spirits visiting

supernaturals was a common thing, a positive thing, or a heart wrenching thing. I had the urge to tell him that I was sorry, but I didn't want to say the wrong thing.

"I just had this weird feeling like I should tell you," Daniel said as he shifted in his seat. "Do you know why I'd have a feeling like that?"

I shook my head slowly, but even as I did the note came to mind. And Al, who Rick knew, also sprang to mind. That coincidence was too major. This was the perfect opportunity to tell Daniel about it. Maybe he'd be able to make heads or tails of it. "Okay, so I did something."

Daniel set his fork down and gave me his full attention.

"I know you know bits and pieces about the strange things I've been experiencing since coming back to Mystic Hollow..."

He smirked but said nothing.

Yeah, strange things was putting it mildly. "Well, I haven't told you everything." I didn't wait for his answer, I just pushed forward. "The first time I suspected I had magic was when my ex and his *affair partner* showed up at my house, stole some of my stuff, and I accidentally turned them into toads. I didn't mean to! I wasn't even sure if I'd actually done it, or if I was losing my mind. But that's why they were missing. And before you say anything, I should have told you about my involvement in his disappearance, but because of your connection to the police, I didn't want to put you in a bad spot. And don't worry, I fixed everything when I went back. They're human again and they don't know what happened."

I stop talking and stare at him.

He cleared his throat and took a sip of his drink. "Okay, I can accept all of that. And I can even forgive you not being completely honest with me. But for future reference, although I'm connected to the police, I'm not a cop any longer. I don't ever think you could do something truly awful, so if you run into trouble, just tell me. Be honest with me. But I don't want you to keep important things from me again. Honesty is really important to me in a relationship."

Relationship?

"Okay." I pushed forward, wanting to tell him everything before it was too late. "But there's more. I've been receiving strange notes here saying that they knew what I did with my husband. Kind of threatening and scary. I haven't been able to figure out who could've done it, but I recently learned from my ex that he has a work buddy that he's close to, and Al, who lives here. I'm thinking he could be the person responsible."

His face froze. "Someone has been leaving you threatening messages?"

"Yeah," I said, feeling uncertain.

He lifted a brow and anger blazed in his eyes. "*That* will get taken care of." He seemed to take a minute, then continued, his anger fading. "But I have to say, I can't see Al being involved in anything like that. He's just not that kind of guy. Why don't we stop by after dinner and be sure though, so we can move onto other suspects?"

I felt strangely relieved. Not only would I get to meet the guy, but Daniel would be there with me. "That sounds wonderful!"

"Now," he picked up his fork again. "Let's finish eating and grab some dessert."

"You're a man after my own heart," I told him.

"I hope so," he said, and took another bite.

I hoped so too.

TWELVE

Emma

We were back in Daniel's loaner truck, with the windows rolled up, and some old rock n' roll playing softly in the background. I probably should have been more stressed out than I was, but Daniel's calming aura had a way of making me feel like I was always safe in his presence.

"So, you really think this guy isn't the culprit? Because everything would finally make sense."

"I'm telling you; Al doesn't have anything to do with the note." Daniel shook his head and peered out the windshield.

"What makes you say that?"

"His personality. He's just a quiet guy who likes his routines. He's also pretty friendly, but also the nervous type. I once saw a pretty girl speak to him, and he literally just blurted the word 'boobs,' and ran."

I grinned. "Boobs?"

"Yup. And once he started babbling to me about a new computer game. I was polite but didn't have a clue what he was talking about. I ended up hearing him call himself stupid over and over again on the way to his car. I felt bad for the guy."

"Okay, he doesn't really sound like the stalking harassment type," I admit, "but I will feel better after we talk to him."

Daniel turned down a street, into a quiet neighborhood. We drove along, each house looking almost identical to the next. Little houses with brown shutters and white siding with almost non-existent front yards with small patches of neatly trimmed grass. Daniel pulled up to one at random, one of the only houses with the lights on inside and turned off the engine.

"Just remember," Daniel said into the silence. "I'm here, and I'll never let anyone hurt you."

"I believe that," I told him, feeling my cheeks heat, and then I opened the door, trying to escape before he noticed the effect his words had on me.

I stepped out of Daniel's shiny loaner truck and led the way to the front door, feeling more confident with him behind me. When he put his hand on the small of my back, I couldn't help but smile. It was a small touch, but it was an intimate one that made me feel cared for in a way I hadn't felt in a long time.

"Al is a night owl, so he's always up, but he never answers his damned phone. I texted him three times. Hopefully he's actually here." Daniel had already me told me as much, but I had a feeling he was talking to try to soothe my nerves. It was a kindness I appreciated.

I froze in front of the door. The house certainly *looked* like someone was home. A light flickered in the front window, like a TV was playing, and I swore I could hear the sound of the TV too.

"Hang on," he whispered and pulled a gun out from somewhere under his jacket.

Um, okay. I hadn't even realized he was packing. But he was a former sheriff. It was probably second nature for him. "What's wrong?" I asked, matching his hushed tone.

"The door." He nodded toward the door which I belatedly realized was ajar.

"Oh, no," I breathed.

Maybe the guy was just forgetful. I'd left the door open a time or two after carrying groceries inside. It didn't mean anything was wrong. Right?

I started to move forward when Daniel grabbed my shoulder with his free hand. "Stay here. Go back to the truck and be prepared to call 911 if I'm not back in a minute or if anything happens. Do not come in after me."

"Maybe it's nothing," I whispered.

His gaze never wavered from the door. "Trust me, it's always better to be safe than sorry."

Tears threatened to fill my eyes as my adrenaline caused my body to react. But I nodded, then did as he asked, hurrying back down the porch steps, and stopping in front of the truck. I turned just in time to see Daniel disappear into the small house.

"Oh, geez," I moaned and shifted my phone from one hand to the other. This whole thing felt strangely ominous. Actually, the house kind of felt ominous. And the realization made my breath catch. A slightly open door might be a reason for an ex-cop like Daniel to be cautious, but this feeling was like the nail in the coffin. I didn't have the ability to read a room like my friends did, but something bad had happened or was happening in that place, my gut was suddenly sure of it. How had I not sensed it before getting to the door?

A ghost appeared in front of me, causing me to squeak, jump, and drop my phone. "Geez!"

I grasped my chest, and looked at him, but he seemed completely unthreatening, like the dancing ghosts I'd met before. So, I tried to ignore the shaking in my legs and bent down, while keeping my eyes on the ghost, and picked up my phone. "Who are you? And what are you doing hanging around here?"

He kept flickering in and out, but when he spoke, at least I was able to hear him. "I'm Thomas," the flickery man said, but the sound cut in and out with his image.

Thomas? *The* Thomas?

"You're Daniel's friend?" I asked.

My gaze moved over him. I'd known Thomas in high school, but not all that well. I'd just constantly seen him, and Daniel attached at the hip. I'd never really paid attention to the guy, because, well, who would notice another man with Daniel around? But now, it kind of surprised me. He looked like a bigger, older version of his son. He even had the same pain in his gray eyes.

"I've been trying to warn you both. I was murdered. The man who did it is after you now."

Wait, murdered, I thought he'd died in a car accident? And the killer was after us? That didn't make any sense.

I opened my mouth to ask him to elaborate, but he flickered again and disappeared.

"What the heck?" I looked all around, but there was no sign of the ghost. "Thomas?" I whisper-yelled.

Daniel came out of the house then, his gun put away. "It's okay, nobody is in there. I cleared the whole place."

I hurried forward. "So, he's okay?"

He winced and pulled out his cell. "No, Al's dead."

Wow. That wasn't good. Not at all. "Recently?"

Daniel nodded gravely as he pressed his phone to his ear. "Yes," he said, then spoke into his phone. "I need to report a dead body."

Leaning back, I rested against the truck. I hadn't even had a chance to tell him about the ghost, and I sure as heck wasn't going to with him on the phone. Telling this man his beloved friend, and, my stomach clenched, the woman he loved, were murdered, was not something to casually tell someone.

This was just terrible. All of this.

What if the murderer who the ghost tried to warn me about was the one who killed Al?

I needed answers, and I needed them now.

THIRTEEN

Emma

"I'm going to run her home," Daniel said to Sheriff Danvers. "I'll be right back." He hated that I was here, involved in yet another crime scene in Mystic Hollow, I could tell from the set of his shoulders and his clipped tone. To say Daniel was protective would be an understatement. There's a reason a man like him joins the police and it's to do with the sense of justice and honor that goes down to the very core of his being, but with that comes a healthy dose of wanting to be everyone's shield.

My neighborhood wasn't far from Al's place, which creeped me out a bit, but at least that meant that Daniel wouldn't be gone long. We walked back to the green truck, and I hopped in. Once both of our doors were shut, I said, "There's something else I need to tell you."

He turned over the engine, so the truck was rumbling quietly underneath us and looked at me warily. "What else?"

"While you were inside the house, a ghost appeared to me. He was almost as tall as you and even though he was a ghost I could tell that in life he had dark hair and a full, busy beard. His eyes seemed really pale gray as well, but I don't know if that was just from him being a ghost or what he actually looked like, and he had a scar on his cheek just here." I pointed to the right side of my face, just over the cheek bone, but slightly off to the side.

Daniel swallowed audibly when he glanced at me and saw where I was pointing before he looked back at the road. "That was Thomas," Daniel said in a soft voice. He glanced at me again when he asked, "He came to you?"

I nodded. "And I think he appeared on my porch as we left for our non-date, but I wasn't sure until I saw him again. I thought at first maybe I was just remembering things I'd seen before, but he looked different from the last ghost."

Daniel pulled off the small street and onto the main road, maneuvering past the police cars that were lining the area. "What did he do?"

"He spoke to me."

Daniel glanced at me in surprise, his eyes which were dark in the evening light going wide. "He did? When he came to me his lips moved but there was no noise."

"Well, this time, he was super flickery, like he couldn't maintain a connection, but I could hear him." Not that I wanted to think about it or was particularly eager to experience it, but seeing ghosts and what not, I couldn't help but wonder what the afterlife was like. Had Thomas been at peace and then sensed a danger to Daniel and came to warn him? Or had he been roaming and restless?

"And what did he say?" Daniel asked, his voice holding something close to hope mixed with curiosity.

"He said he was murdered, and the man who murdered him is now after me."

Daniel was quiet for a long time, long enough that I was

about to ask him if he was okay when he said, "Damn. I'm glad I asked for someone to watch your house."

I looked in the side mirror and saw a police car following us. My heart sank. Since I'd become Karma, I'd been nothing but trouble to those around me. But I had to take the bad with the good. I wouldn't have rekindled my friendships with my friends or learned what I now knew about them and their powers, either.

If I hadn't become Karma I would probably still be in Springfield and drinking myself into an early grave. My heart would have remained forever broken, my ability to trust would have been crushed, and I would have pulled away from the world. I can almost see it in my mind, exactly how life would have gone. My divorce with Rick would have been long and messy and painful, and whatever job I ended up getting would have just been a means to an end. I would have been lost.

Becoming Karma and reuniting with my chosen family in Mystic Hollow grounded me, centered me in a way I didn't even know I was lacking. It made me see things in a new light, everything from my old life to my current self. If I hadn't become Karma that never would have happened.

In my driveway, Daniel turned off the truck, making everything quiet, which was the only thing that pulled me from my thoughts. "Please be careful," he said. "I know you have powers but this... That murder was strange, to say the least." He shuddered. "I don't believe it was done by a human."

That wasn't good news. I grabbed his hand. "I'll be careful. I promise." Squeezing his fingers, I waited for him to explain, but he shook his head.

"I'll explain everything when I know more."

After seriously considering pressing a kiss to his cheek, I

gave it up and slid out of the truck. He didn't open my door this time, which was understandable. I only turned back once to say, "You be careful, too."

He gave me a nod in response and when Daniel pulled out of my driveway, the officer pulled in. I waved, ignoring the guilt that meant another cop had to sit in my driveway all night. I tried to reframe it in my mind, he would have been bored or in danger otherwise, right? I wasn't convinced that this murderer was going to come after me immediately, so that meant that being here made the officer safe and he wasn't just sitting at the station, so it had to be more entertaining, right? Maybe that was naive, but I thought one murder a night was probably all the killer was capable of.

Besides, my brother was inside. So, even if I wasn't in danger, I was glad to know he'd be extra safe.

Henry looked up when I locked the door. "Hey," I said. "How's it going?"

He grinned and took off his headset, moving away from where he'd been reading something at the kitchen table. "Good timing. I was about to take a break." He followed me into the kitchen watching intensely as I set the kettle to boil and got out the stuff for tea. "Want some?" I asked, waggling my mug at him.

He nodded his head, so I reached for a second mug and tea bag. I knew he could tell that something was up, and he was just waiting for me to come out with it. I wasn't sure that I wanted to though, I mean what if it put him in danger? But what if not knowing put him in danger, too? I decided knowing was better than not knowing.

"I had a rough night," I said, not really knowing how to tell him that yet another person I'm tangentially connected to has died.

"Oh?" Henry cocked his head, the dark brown strands

that looked black most of the time brushing over his fore-head almost hiding his furrowed brow. "Can I help you?"

I turned so I was facing him fully and reached up to tousle his hair. As soon as I removed my hand from his hair, he straightened it back out with a slight smile and went to sit at the table. A lot of people thought Henry didn't like to be touched, but he did. Just only by a few trusted people. As a kid, he would cringe from the hugs and kisses from relatives, which always annoyed them. But he seemed to enjoy the small things I did, like tousling his hair, or giving him little hugs and kisses. I was always careful not to give long hugs though, those he didn't enjoy.

Gosh, it was nice to be home and back with him. I hadn't even realized just how much I missed all the little things that made him my Henry.

I cleared my throat, trying to hide my sappy thoughts as I said, "Just make sure you're being safe. Don't go outside at night right now, lock everything up. Someone is murdering people in town, and I don't want it to be you."

I didn't want to freak him out, but he had to know the danger. After I set a mug of tea in front of him, Henry grabbed my hand. "Are you really okay?"

Giving him a half hug, I chuckled. "I'm fine. We have an officer watching the house just to be safe." It was time to change the subject. "What are you playing?" I released him from the hug and moved to sit on the other side of the table with my own mug, letting the heat warm my hands and chase away the nerves of the evening.

It was a pretty safe bet that he was playing something, he just changed the subject matter and team from time to time, though I had a feeling Alice would always be a staple now. "I've been playing this sandbox game for a while that was recently updated, and some friends and I are crushing the game." He grinned before taking a sip of the tea and burning his mouth. I couldn't help but shake my head as he waved a hand over his tongue.

I eyed him over the rim of the mug as I took a sip. He seemed genuinely relaxed and happy, which I loved to see but I needed to make sure of one thing first. When I put the mug back down, I asked, "You're not gambling are you?" My stomach was tight as I waited for his response. The last thing I needed to worry about right now was my brother getting in trouble with vampires and sirens again.

He shook his head hard, his hair flying all over. "No, not since I got in trouble. Not even a little. It's just me and five geniuses crushing this game."

I relaxed. My brother was a good man. He'd just made a misstep. "Good to hear." After finishing my tea and giving him a kiss on the cheek, I took off for bed. I was beyond exhausted. I just hoped there wasn't a ghost waiting for me in my bedroom or something.

FOURTEEN

Emma

"Come on," Beth said over my phone's speaker. "We heard about the murder. Meet us at Deva's for breakfast." Did she have to be so peppy this early in the morning?

Yeah, of course she did. Beth was always peppy. While I felt like a pile of day-old porridge.

"Urgh," I mumbled. I hadn't even cracked an eye yet. When Beth called, I slapped at my phone until it actually answered the call. I'd been trying to reject it but whatever. I was awake now. I coughed a few times as I tried to get my voice to work properly before I managed to say, "I'll be there in about a half hour."

What I wanted, no, needed, to do was sit and soak in a bathtub with one of those fizzy bombs that makes the water all pretty and smells divine, then shave and lotion and wash away my cares of the last three and a half weeks.

What I actually did was run a brush through my hair, spray some dry shampoo in it, wipe myself down in the sink really quick, and wash my face, before putting on some deodorant and perfume. Finally, I left the house ten minutes later looking like a somewhat normal human and smelling like... well, hopefully like nothing, or the perfume at worst. I didn't think my friends would judge me, especially based on my last twenty-four hours, but other people might, and I had no idea what the day had in store for me yet.

A different officer sat in my driveway. This one was younger, and more...shiny. Like he was a brand-new penny. I walked up to his window and bent over. "I'm going to Deva's Delights. If you need to follow me, feel free, I'll have some of Deva's famous pancakes sent out for you. Or you can stay here and keep an eye on Henry. But be warned, he's like me. *Not* a morning person."

His dark eyes sparkled with excitement as he gave me a broad grin. "Deva's it is." I knew Deva's food was legendary for so many reasons, but seeing other people react to it like that made me so happy for my friend, not to mention proud. This was her dream, her work, her blood, sweat, and tears going into making her place a reality. Though not into the food. She was meticulously clean.

He backed out into the street and let me pull my car onto the road in front of him, then followed me to Deva's place. The whole time my sluggish mind was begging me for a cup of coffee while also starting to mull over the events of last night. And not just the murder but spending time with Daniel and have it be so...nice. And that wasn't damning it with faint praise either. I couldn't remember the last time I'd spent time with a man like him and thought it was nice. I was always counting the seconds until I could excuse myself or feign a headache or something. Last night I hadn't wanted to leave.

I'd been able to snag a parking spot right out front and as soon as I walked in, I spotted Beth and Carol at a table near the front window, they weren't quite visible from outside, but they had a view of the whole place. The hostess greeted me, and I asked, "Can you send a to-go box of Deva's pancakes, fully loaded, and a big cup of tea and another big cup of coffee, out to the officer out front, please?" I gestured to the patrol car across the street as the hostess pulled out a small notebook and wrote the order down. When she was finished, I added, "Just add it to my bill." I hoped that he liked tea or coffee because that's all he was getting to choose from.

She smiled widely at me. "Of course. Right away."

"Hey ladies," I called as I wove through the other tables to my friends.

They stood. Beth gave me a hug when I was close enough. "Hey," Carol said. "Let's go find Deva and you can fill us in, that way you don't have to tell the story over and over again."

All of the wait staff and cooks knew us, so no one stopped us from heading to the back, but when we walked into the kitchen, it was to find Deva smiling broadly up at Marquis. I stopped short and Beth and Carol thumped into my back. "What is it?" Carol asked, peering over my shoulder. "Oh," she said with a sigh that almost sounded wistful. "How nice."

The three of us backpedaled and returned to the table they'd claimed. "So, tell us the details," Beth said. "We'll fill Deva in later. I'm sure she'd rather be with Marquis."

"I'm so happy for her," I said as my friends grabbed bags they had stashed under the table. As I told them what had happened on my not-date with Daniel last night, they pulled out old high school yearbooks. Thankfully they just had three each, I assumed one on each side of the four years we were in school, though where they got them, I had no idea. Still, I was glad they came prepared.

"Let's see if we can find this Al," Carol said as she flipped open the first yearbook, the hard, fancy cover making a knocking sound as it hit the table. The glossy black and white pages flipped before us as Carol scanned through the book. We were all focusing on one book so if any of us missed him hopefully the others would catch him. It made it take longer but it felt more thorough.

It took a few minutes of searching, but finally Beth's finger landed next to a photo, as she tapped at the book and exclaimed, "Here he is! And it's so weird. He was in our class."

I scooted closer to peer down at the guy from the right angle. "How is that possible? I don't remember his face at all."

"Me either," Carol said. "Not even a wiggle of a memory." And we had a small high school. Maybe seventy in our graduating class. No way there was a member of it at least one of us didn't remember. It made me doubt my memories, since it was more likely they were wrong than the yearbook.

"Maybe Deva will remember him," I said.

But Deva didn't remember. She walked out looking blissfully happy and carrying a tray full of plates. We hadn't even ordered, but that didn't surprise me. It wasn't just Deva's food that was magical, it was the way she always seemed to know what we'd want, what would help us most in that moment. The tray was laden with fruit salad, eggs, muffins, and other little yummy bites that I didn't have a name for.

"How was that?" I asked with a broad grin.

Deva set the plates down and handed the empty tray off to one of the staff before she sat down herself and joined us.

"Um, I told him I couldn't go to brunch with him because my morning prep guy called out sick. Marquis showed up and did prep with me. He wouldn't take no for an answer, and you know what? He made it faster and a lot easier."

"I bet the time passed very quickly," Beth said slyly as she dug into her omelet. The undertone to her comment was definitely not missed. By anyone. Which was most evident by the slight blush that stained Deva's cheeks.

We ate and discussed Al, who Deva didn't remember either. The whole thing was giving me the creeps.

"Okay," Deva said. "What we need to do is split up and go talk to someone from all the cliques in our graduating class. Obviously, Daniel knew Al. We need to ask everyone else. Joel ran around with the gearheads and owns the mechanic's shop now. I know him, so I can go ask him."

"I know Cindy, she was on the volleyball team and head cheerleader," Beth said. "She comes in the shop a lot."

"We were kind of on the fringes," I said. "Joel covers the kids from the auto body shop. The jocks will be covered by Cindy." We kept naming names until each of us had two or three people to see. The goths, the smokers. The brains. The band nerds. Pretty much every clique we could come up with, and then we combed the yearbooks for more.

We had a good list to go on now. Time to investigate. I couldn't say I was excited about the prospect of an impromptu class reunion, even if it was on an individual basis. There was just something about catching up with people from high school, people who knew you when you had the most potential, that made me feel icky. When I thought about it, I felt like I'd failed a little bit.

I'd moved out of town, left Mystic Hollow, which was what most of the high school students wanted to do at some point or another, and now I was back because my marriage had fallen apart. It wouldn't matter that my ex was a cheating jerk or that I was happier in Mystic Hollow, they'd see me, one of the few people that had actually left and had come back, and I knew that they'd be wondering what the heck happened. How did I screw up my perfect life?

The problem is that life was only perfect when it was being observed by strangers. Anyone who actually knew me would be able to see how unhappy I had been, and they should be able to see how much happier I was being back home. I just wasn't excited about the prospect of having to recap my life to multiple people and seeing the pity and judgement in their eyes. Maybe I'd be wrong though? Maybe more people would understand it than I thought. That was my hope anyway.

All I had to do was navigate that and figure out who knew Al. I couldn't say my life wasn't interesting, sometimes I wished it wasn't full of so many questions though. The primary one currently being who the heck even was Al?

FIFTEEN

Daniel

A sense of impending doom had me on my front porch, sniffing the air and waiting for whatever was about to happen. Sometimes, as shifters, we sensed stuff like this. And yet, as I scanned the area I deemed my front yard, I saw nothing that should have my bear so upset. My gaze went to the woods all around me, and I strained to see or smell anything that might be off. Everything seemed to be in its place.

But that just meant I hadn't found the source of my unease yet.

Narrowing my eyes, I locked my door and took a few steps down from my porch. Sniffing the area slowly and feeling every hair on my body stand on end. A slow growl rolled up my throat, and the territorial instinct deep inside me rumbled through my mind and body.

Someone or something was on my land.

I took a few more steps, sniffing the air, then froze. I smelled Nathan. This wasn't good. I hadn't realized he'd gotten sprung from the county already. The fact that he was here now probably meant he was itching for a fight. The bear within me wanted that fight. He wanted to show the pup that he couldn't just show up on my lands and expect to be welcome, not after the fury he had shown at our last meeting. But I wasn't a young man who gave into my bear's wants over my own any longer. If this kid was looking for a fight, I'd do everything in my power to make sure he didn't get it from me.

I shifted quickly and headed in the direction I'd smelled him. It didn't take me long to find him. He was near the house rather than far out in the woods like I half expected. He'd driven halfway up my road, pulled off, and shifted. I still caught whiffs of exhaust fumes from him. It didn't make a lot of sense to me. I'd expect him to taunt me at the edge of my lands, but not be foolish enough to be smack dab in my territory.

With any other shifter, that would be a dangerous move on his part. Either he didn't care, or this was something else.

His gray eyes met mine as he stood near his truck, but there was nothing defensive in his position. Instead, he seemed uncertain as he turned his back on me and trotted into the woods. His dark fur, the same shade as his hair, was a little messy and tangled. As I followed him, it half made me wonder if he'd gone directly from jail to see me, which probably wasn't a good thing. He hadn't even given his temper a chance to cool.

His wolf stopped in the woods and shifted into the young man I'd been so worried about. And sure enough, he looked like a mess. There was no way he'd had a chance to shower since jail, not with the dirt on his face, and his hair a mess. And yet, he wasn't radiating rage.

He wasn't radiating anything that my bear could pick up on, which made me even more uneasy. Animals were good at reading non-verbal cues. I should be certain right now of how he felt.

So, I didn't shift yet. I was certainly safer in this form if things got messy. A bear could just pin him down and let him work out his anger, without injuring him too terribly.

"I dreamed about my dad," Nathan said, kicking the dirt with his toes.

Okay. If I had to guess, I'd say he hadn't dreamed of his father. His father's ghost had probably visited him. But it was enough to make me shift back. Or maybe the reason I shifted back was because, when he looked up at me again, that deep hurt was back in his eyes.

I stood, shaking myself a little, then met his gaze once more. "Tell me about it."

Nathan looked around, and not seeing anywhere to sit, plopped down on the dirt. It was a subtle way he was showing me deference. Something hard for an alpha to do.

I released a slow breath. He wasn't looking for a fight. He was looking to talk. That, I could handle.

"It started in jail. My roommate was an old badger. Literally. He was a badger shifter."

I raised my eyebrows. "Don't see them around much."

But in this town, I knew exactly who he was talking about. I didn't know him well. Prey animals tended to stay away from large predators. And the fact that he was well-known for his drunken mistakes... he had even more of a reason to stay away from an ex-cop. But I knew him well enough to picture the tiny old man, with a few wisps of grey hair, and wild eyes.

Nathan nodded after a moment. "He was only there for a night, but he told me that he and I are a lot alike. He'd heard of me." Nathan stared off into the forest and scoffed.

"He said it like he was proud of it. He wanted me to be like him."

I didn't reply. He'd obviously seen himself in the older man, too, and hadn't liked what he saw. Sometimes the worst thing, and the best thing, we can do when we're making bad choices is to hold a mirror up to ourselves. It can feel like a crushing blow to see the truth in a way that we couldn't ignore, but it often saved people. I'd seen that time and again as a cop, and I'd seen it when I was at my lowest point.

"Anyway, that got me a little shook up. Then I dreamed about Dad."

I didn't tell him what I suspected, just let him get it all out.

"Dad told me I was wasting my potential and that he was proud of me, but that I needed to straighten up before I ruined it all."

Nathan looked up at me with sorrow in his big gray eyes. "I want to change. I want to be a good leader and take our pack higher, not lower."

Smiling, I stepped forward and sat across from the boy. "I'm really happy to hear that." I kept my happiness in check, though. Nathan had talked about the straight and narrow before and nothing had come of it. This time did seem more serious, more sincere, but I'd proceed with caution and see what happened.

"I'm here for you, Nathan," I said. "In any capacity. Advice, anything. You know that don't you?"

He nodded. "Yeah. That's one thing you've always made clear."

I swallowed around the lump in my throat. "When... when we lost him, I struggled in my own way too."

"You didn't seem to," he said, and there was no malice in his voice.

"Losing Sarah and him broke me," I told him honestly. "But I didn't want to stay broken forever, so I had to force myself to make good choices. It was really, really hard at first. Remember to eat. Remember to sleep. Exercise. Smile. Talk to someone. It felt like things that were easy for other people were horribly difficult for me. But with time, it got easier. Until finally, I started to feel normal again."

"Did," he froze, looked spooked for a second, then pressed on, "did the pain ever go away?"

I opened my mouth to say the same thing I told others when they asked, but I stopped, then spoke the truth. "Not completely. It's like there are a couple doors in my heart where those rooms of pain are, but they keep getting smaller, and I'm getting other rooms in my heart, ones that aren't filled with pain."

He rubbed his chest. "I hope I feel that way sometime."

"You will," I promise, "but it takes work. People say it just takes time, but they're wrong, there's work too."

"I can work," he said, softly.

"I know you can."

He looked at his hands. "When my uncle became my guardian, I wanted it to be you instead."

Damn it. I'd never told the kid, because I figured as a young teenager who had lost his parents, it was already too much for him, but now I saw my chance to clear some things up. "I was a mess, but I still fought for your guardianship. Your dad had made it clear to me, he wanted me to raise you if anything happened, but your uncle went the legal route. And he didn't want me anywhere near you. I did my best, but... I didn't want to be cut off completely from the pack."

He pulled his knees to his chest, looking so young. "I know you think I'm the reason the pack has nothing, but he left me almost nothing to work with. All he did was drink and spend the pack money. As soon as I turned eighteen, I kicked him out. Not that he minded. The money was gone, and he liked being a rogue wolf."

I knew the guy was drinking a lot and not adding to the pack, but I didn't know it was that bad. "Why didn't you tell me?"

He shrugged. "Probably the same reason you didn't tell me that you fought for me. There was nothing either of us could do about it."

I hated that he was right. It would've taken a lot of proof to convince a court that a grieving widower with no familial ties to Nathan was a better guardian than his uncle. Even if I could convince them that his drunken uncle wasn't a safe choice, Nathan probably would have just been sent into foster care, split up from his pack, and that would have been the worst thing I could have done to him.

He gave a little nod and looked at me again. "If you don't mind, could we have dinner one night soon? Talk about the direction of my pack?"

Don't be too eager!

Slowly, I stood and held out my hand to the boy. "I'd like that. I'll text you and make steaks and potatoes."

He grinned and took my hand. "I always loved your cooking." I was the only shifter Thomas really let Nathan around. A mistake, in retrospect.

I helped him to his feet. And I must be a glutton for punishment, but I actually thought there was a new light in his eyes. "I can teach you. If you want."

"I'd like that. The pack is getting pretty tired of fast

food," he grinned, released my hand, and turned to head back to his truck.

So, much potential...

As he walked away, one worry lifted off of my heart and I hoped fervently that his father had heard it all. "I miss you buddy," I muttered as I headed back to my house.

When I opened my front door, it hit me. The musty smell of a goblin. He must have done something to mask his scent until this moment, which was concerning. Instantly on my guard, I almost shifted, but a man walked out of my kitchen holding a sandwich. What the hell?

"Don't shift," he said. Not a man. A goblin. He let his true face flash at me. Beneath an average face, with brown hair, brown eyes, and thick cheeks, was a green face. No hair, no brows, and a narrow nose and beady dark eyes.

"What do you want?" I asked guardedly, my bear growling within me. A younger me would have killed this creature for so brazenly entering my home and my territory, but the older me hesitated. I'd only heard of a goblin visiting a shifter in stories and it was supposedly many, many years ago.

"I have information that you need."

"There's something called a phone..." I growled.

He stiffened. "Calm, shifter. I'm here to help, and this could only be done in person. If I'm wrong, you can tear me to pieces."

"Agreed." The word rumbled from my chest.

He set his sandwich on the coffee table and grabbed a manila envelope. Opening it up, he carefully set the contents of it down.

They were pictures of a crime scene. That was for sure. I inched toward them, while trying not to take my eye off of him for too long.

When he was done, he picked up his sandwich again. "Someone didn't want this ghost talking."

I gaped at the photos. There was a body in the center of the floor and symbols all around it. Organs had been placed at different areas near the symbols, and an antique goblet near his head seemed to contain blood... and a couple eyes.

In my time on the force, handling supernatural crimes, I'd seen some grisly scenes. Most of the time, I could recognize the spell almost instantly. But... I'd never seen anything like this before.

"Who or what could have performed such a spell?" I asked.

This looked so deliberate, like all spells. But the carving up of the body and organs took it from a simple spell to something darker and more dangerous. Something I'd only ever read about. Doing a spell like this would take someone powerful and twisted.

"Few people are capable of this. So, it had to be someone dangerous. Dangerous enough that more than shifters and witches should be scared," the goblin said around a mouth full of ham, lettuce, and tomato. "Which isn't good."

He wasn't wrong. This wasn't good, not at all.

SIXTEEN

Emma

The man was going on and on. No matter what we did, he wouldn't stop. We were supposed to be rapidly going through the names on our list to figure out our suspects, but we'd realized this man wasn't a bad guy within a minute. We couldn't keep wasting time with him, but I was starting to think the only way out was to scream and run for it.

We have to get out of here, good grief! I exchanged another frustrated glance with Carol. She and I had decided to tag team part of our list, while Beth and Deva hit their part of the list.

We'd made it to our second-to-last name on the list, but he was a dud. And now as we kept trying to get into the car, he wouldn't stop talking to us. "Yeah, I was about two years below you in school," he said. "What a good time we always had."

"Yeah," I said, even though all I remembered about him was that he was tiny, talkative, and odd then too. I'd always been polite, but he'd drive me a bit crazy then too.

I guess that hadn't changed.

"Well, we should—" Carol tried to say we should leave, but he interrupted her.

"You know, a lot of my crew had a crush on you, Emma," he stuffed his hands in his pockets and kicked the ground a little. "But you had to go and marry an out of towner. You broke a lot of hearts."

Me? I hadn't been popular at all! What was this guy talking about? "Um, I didn't know that." I shouldn't have said that. I should've said goodbye.

"Well, you were human," he said. "And off limits. Though some of the guys seriously considered breaking the rules for you. We even had a conversation back then about telling you about our world."

Man, I tried to picture them telling me about all this as a teenager. I probably would have just thought they were on drugs. Still, if I said that now, I had a feeling he'd launch into a discussion about drugs.

"Well," I said brightly. "It was nice to see you."

He tried to say something else, but I looked away and talked right over him, hoping that he wouldn't take the snub too harshly. We really were in a hurry though. "Hope to run into you soon, but we've got to go!"

Carol and I dove into the car before he could push us to talk about something else. He was still talking as we drove away, waving, with smiles plastered on our faces. He followed us for a few steps before he seemed to relent and just wave back. He seemed lonely, as though we were the first people he'd talked to in days, even though I doubted that was the case. Still if you never had any meaningful conversations then sometimes it felt like you could make up for it with the quantity instead.

"Geez," Carol said when we pulled out of the neighborhood. "Jackson is a good guy, but the brownie part of him overwhelms his mouth and he talks incessantly."

"Ohhh," I said. "I wondered what he was, but I wasn't sure how much it would matter since he didn't strike me as the murdering type."

Carol snorted. "No, he definitely isn't. He's annoying but Jackson is harmless. I mean, I wasn't 100% sure until we came into his house and saw his collection of porcelain cows, and his pile of unfinished novels. I figured avoiding the talkative guy at the store wasn't the complete picture of who he was, but... it was."

I laughed. "Yeah, he's sweet. A little annoying, but it wouldn't matter if we weren't in a hurry."

"I actually have a friend who might be a good match for him..." Carol said, voice trailing off. "She's really quiet but always says how she likes to hear people talk."

"Call her. Call her now," I said, and then we were both grinning.

And yet, it wasn't time to worry about the brownie's love life right now. Karma might have to find him someone soon, because he seemed like he deserved a nice person in his life.

As we stopped at a light, I actually looked back and lifted a hand. Closing my eyes, I encouraged my magic toward him. I didn't know what life he deserved, or what kind of man he was, but Karma would figure it out. A slow tingle moved over my flesh, and the scent of books came over me, and then it was gone. Who knows maybe he'd become a famous novelist and have to give lots of interviews about his life? Or maybe all his books will disintegrate into ash? It all depended on what type of person he was and the life he's led.

"Green light," Carol said, and her voice said she knew exactly what I was doing.

I opened my eyes and started driving again, being careful not to let the lingering tingles of using my magic distract me.

"Who's next?" I asked as I pulled into the gas station parking lot a few blocks away. I hoped we were far enough that Jackson couldn't walk here while we pumped gas.

Carol got out and went over our notes. "I got texts from Deva and Carol. They both hit dead ends. All duds, nobody who even remotely seemed suspicious."

I sighed and finished pumping the gas. "Don't we have one more name?"

Carol grimaced. "Louisa. That girl who was always sitting by herself and never talked to anyone."

Her face popped into my mind. "Oh, I always felt so bad for her. She was chubby and had acne and it looked like she never washed her hair. Now, as an adult, I have to wonder what her home life was like. At the time, I just assumed she was kind of gross." I frowned, feeling bad that I hadn't understood back then.

One of the bright spots about being older is that we learn and can do better.

"I know," Carol said. "We were never the bullying type, but I do remember that all we did was try to reach out to her a few times. I feel like we could've done more."

I'd never really even tried to reach out. I hadn't been mean, but I also hadn't been welcoming. Wherever she ended up now, I'd try to be friendly.

"Turn here," Carol said, pointing.

I turned.

"Any idea what she's like now?"

Carol pointed again, and I turned down another road.

"I've seen her, but not spoken to her. I've never been sure if she's not friendly, or just shy." Made sense. We were a small town, but it didn't mean we were all close.

"And pull in here," Carol said.

We pulled up at the animal shelter. "This is where she works?" I asked.

Carol nodded. "Yeah, she's the animal control officer for the county. Since we're full of shifters, we don't need much animal controlling. She probably doesn't get much done."

We walked in to find Louisa sitting behind a desk off to one side, clicking boredly on a computer mouse. The whole place almost had a doctor's office feel to it, with waiting chairs and magazines and that same tile floor that so many businesses around here seemed to have. There was a small room a bit bigger than a walk-in closet off to the other side with a big window and door making up most of it. A sign on the door said, "Get to Know You Room" and two chairs sat inside along with some dog toys.

"Adopt or surrender," she droned when we stepped through the door. The distant sound of a dog barking muffled our footsteps on the hard floor.

"Neither," I said. "We were looking for you, Louisa."

She looked up with interest, but a second after she laid eyes on us, her face hardened, and a sneer curled her lips. "Emma Foxx and Carol Hart. To *what* do I owe the pleasure?"

Whoa. Her voice dripped with sarcasm. It was definitely not a pleasure for Louisa to see us.

"We're trying to figure out if anyone knew this man," I said. Carol held out the yearbook. We'd put a sticky note under Al's face with arrows pointing to his picture to show the people we'd been questioning.

Louisa gave it a quick glance. "No. Is that all?"

"Are you sure? We had a small graduating class, but no one seems to know him."

She didn't bother looking up again. "No. Now, get out."

Get out? What the heck?

"I'm sorry," I said. "Have we done something to offend you?"

Louisa rose from the desk, her belly prominent in her animal control officer's uniform. It almost looked like a police officer's uniform, but there were subtle differences. The main one being that it was olive green. She even had the walkie-talkie radio thingy on her shoulder, even though she appeared to be the only one around. "You were horrible to me in high school."

Carol and I exchanged a surprised glance. "Um," I said. "That's not how I remember it."

Her face darkened. Before she could reply, her cell rang, and instead of quieting it or asking us to give her a moment, she held up one finger and answered. "Hey, sweetie!"

After a few seconds, she kept talking, her finger still in the air, as if we were bugging her to hurry when we were just standing there. "Yeah, they're taking forever with my car. I know. It's awful." Another pause, finger still up. "Sure, come pick me up. My shift ends at six. See you then!"

She hung up and her cheerful tone disappeared. At least she lowered her finger. "Are we done?"

I still didn't know what we'd done to offend her. "If you don't know Al, then yeah, I guess we are. Whatever we did to you in high school, Louisa, I'm sorry."

She glanced at both of us. "Too little, too late."

We walked out as Louisa rounded the desk. She slammed the door shut behind us and locked it.

I looked at Carol in shock. Whoa.

That was our whole list. And everyone had been a dud, except for hateful Louisa. She could've been a suspect, but more likely she was just bitter.

SEVENTEEN

Emma

"Here." Henry handed me a glass; condensation made the glass slick, so I was careful as I took it from him. "I made lemonade." The pale-yellow liquid made me thirsty just looking at it. He'd even put a half slice of fresh lemon on top, which he knew I liked.

"Oh, thanks," I said as he sat beside me on the back deck glider. I was beyond exhausted. I hadn't caught up on my sleep from all the packing and moving, then all this running around town today and the stress of it all... I just needed a month's worth of Sunday naps. At once.

Every bone in my body told me exactly how old I was. My hip, which had never been the same after having Travis, kept protesting my sitting in the old, hard glider and my back was aching in a way that said there almost no possible position in which I could be comfy. It was enough to make me want to go straight to bed, but I was still too wired after everything that had happened.

Why couldn't middle age come with a bubble?

But, oh well. It didn't.

Henry sat quietly for a while, then started telling me about his video game. I tried really hard to focus but poor Henry really droned on about some sort of 'boss' and a raid they were going on later. There was too much detail in what he was telling me for me to really understand it. I needed big picture, bullet point type stuff and he was out in the weeds telling me which was which.

Before things got awkward with Henry and the conversation about his video game, Thomas appeared. "Oh," I said and sat up straight, almost spilling my lemonade down my top, prepared to step in front of Henry if this freaked him out too much. I never knew which way surprises were going to go with him, it just seemed to depend on how much other stuff he'd been dealing with that day, most of which I never knew about.

"Hello," Henry said, cool as a cucumber. "Who are you?" I did a double take at my brother, how was he not freaked out by this? I mean yes, he knew about vampires and shifters and sirens, but had he seen a ghost before? If he had, why on earth hadn't he told me about it? I was learning more about my brother every day it seemed.

Thomas grimaced like he was in pain, his body, or spirit, or whatever you want to call it seemed tense. "Someone is trying to summon me, almost constantly. And someone else is trying to repel me, almost constantly," he said. It looked like he took a deep breath and braced himself but the air around him was still.

"That explains the flickering," I said.

Thomas nodded, then flickered in and out for a moment like an old TV before disappearing for about two seconds. Before Henry or I could open our mouths to question the ghost's appearance, Thomas reappeared.

"Every time they war against each other, it hurts,"

Thomas said through thin lips. He was fully wincing now, and I couldn't imagine what it was taking for him to be here and not give in to one of the parties that seemed to be trying to control him.

"Who?" I cried. "Who is it? I can stop them." I was pretty sure I could, anyway. I'd certainly try my hardest. Just seeing someone in that much pain was difficult, and to know that it was someone that my friends cared about, especially Daniel? I'd kick butt and take names then do whatever I could to make sure Thomas could rest in peace again, or for the first time since I wasn't really sure what had happened.

"I'm forbidden from saying, cursed. I can't speak either name. But there will be more murders if you don't find them and find them fast!" He flickered again this time for longer before disappearing for three seconds this time.

"Is he gone?" I asked, but then Thomas appeared again, several feet away. Henry and I both jumped up and stepped toward him. This time he was flickering almost constantly, his words coming through in fits and starts. He sounded almost like a CD skipping, "Th this person has-s m-m-mmmurder created b-b-before. Th-th-the s-s-s-secrets-s-s a-a-are b-b-buri-i-ied."

He flickered more strongly and then was gone the longest time yet, maybe ten or twelve seconds. As I was beginning to think he was gone for good, he appeared. "I-i-it's a-a-all-l-l a-a-a-bout his-s-story-y-y a-a-nd m-m-math-th-th," he said.

"I have no idea what that means," I cried. "You've got to tell me more."

But this time, when he flickered out, it was almost like there was a pop and he didn't return.

Henry and I stood at the edge of the deck for several

minutes, but then my brother finally sighed. "Ghosts are always talking in riddles." He picked up our cups as I stared at him in surprise. What was that supposed to mean?

"When have you seen ghosts?" I asked. I was genuinely curious and debating about having a full-on sit down with him once I'd had a chance to catch my breath from everything. I needed to know what he knew about the supernatural world, and what he didn't. It would help me protect him in the future.

He didn't directly answer me though, as was often his way. "When I play my game, I'm always a mage, and my ghost friends always talk in riddles."

Maybe he'd just meant his game. Perhaps he was so used to ghosts in his fictional world that he'd been okay with Thomas in this one. That had to be right, didn't it?

I just needed someone to tell me that he hadn't been able to see ghosts his whole life and been unable to tell me. If he had been dealing with this and felt like he couldn't talk to me? I wasn't sure I'd be able to handle that. Maybe he saw ghosts all the time though? Maybe this was just an average Tuesday to him?

All I knew was that my head was spinning and as Henry disappeared inside with the glasses I wasn't sure what to do next. How could I track down this murderer and protect my brother and help Thomas? It was too much.

EIGHTEEN

Emma

Even though I was beyond exhausted, I called my girls, and they came right over. Henry was lost in his online world, apparently going on the raid he mentioned earlier, as we sat around the kitchen table, and I told them about the ghost.

"I think it's time to visit the graveyard," Deva said, "Maybe with the four of us, and the fact that this is a full moon, we'll be able to get someone from the beyond who knows what the heck is going on."

Beth and Carol exchanged glances with me, eyebrows raised, like, why not? I mean I could think of a few reasons, for one, I was exhausted, for another, there was a murderer on the loose, wouldn't going to a graveyard kind of give him an easy place to hide the bodies?

They seemed pretty gung-ho about it even though I yawned. I sighed and said, "Okay, but as soon as this is settled, I'm sleeping for a month."

"Deal," Carol said. "You deserve it."

"I think we all do," Beth mumbled as she caught my

yawn. She stretched as she stood before shaking herself awake once more.

"So," I started slowly, "was Mystic Hollow *always* this interesting?"

Beth shook her head, brows drawing together. "No, there have always been issues, which is why my business stays so busy, but you've definitely brought some chaos into Mystic Hollow."

I felt a little guilt. "Sorry."

Deva smiled. "It's not your fault. Besides, life was getting a little boring before you showed up."

"What you all wouldn't give for *boring* now, huh?"

They laughed.

We had a conversation with the officer, telling him our plan, before piling into Deva's car after. He agreed to follow us to the entrance to the cemetery, but then leave us be so we could do our thing. He winked, making me think he knew about the supernatural side of life. Most of the police force in Mystic Hollow did. In their line of work, they saw too much to not realize there was more to this world.

We pulled into the cemetery and true to his word, Officer McCoy parked at the entrance. He'd also promised not to let anyone in, so it wasn't a complete surprise when his patrol car literally parked across the entrance. This particular graveyard had a private area in the back with benches and only one way in or out, unless by woods.

The sun was just starting to set as we pulled around the bend and parked by the 'contemplation gardens.'

Nobody wanted to contemplate with the dead. Grieve, sure. Summon, sometimes. Contemplate? Not so much.

"Okay, so what's the deal?" I asked. "What are we doing?"

"Well, we need to summon some ghosts," Deva said.

"Easier said than done, but it's a new moon and near the autumn solstice. We'll be able to pull extra power from the moon."

We sat in a circle and let Beth lead. She felt like she could do this, so heck, I was happy to let her try.

"All you have to do is relax," she said.

I chuckled. "If I relax too much I'll just sleep, and you can do whatever you need to." It felt like lately I had two modes: sleep or running around like a chicken with my head cut off.

Wait, were we going to need a blood sacrifice to raise the dead? Isn't that what they needed whenever they showed it on the TV or in movies? No, they would have said something if that was the case, right?

We grinned but then quieted down to let Beth focus. I relaxed as much as I could, jumping a little when I felt Beth tap into my powers and draw on them. It tickled.

But I didn't close my eyes. That really would have resulted in me sleeping.

Since I was the only one with my eyes open, I was the first to gasp, and then laugh when the ghost of a little skunk toddled toward us. Its large butt was swaying heavily as it waddled, and I couldn't help but wonder if a ghost skunk could make me stink like a real skunk? If they could, this was about to be a very short attempt at summoning the dead.

"Well, hello there," Beth said once she opened her eyes, practically cooing at the animal. "Who are you?"

The skunk cocked its head and looked up at her, then spoke in the deepest, grouchiest voice I'd ever heard. If Danny DeVito was an animal, he would've been this skunk's voice. "What's the big idea? I was happy!"

"Sorry," Beth yelped, then the itchy feeling of her drawing on my magic disappeared. So, did the skunk.

"Maybe I'll lead the circle," Carol said.

"I don't think that's going to be enough," Deva said, glancing at me, then back to Carol. "I think we're going to have to lean into it."

I arched one eyebrow. "What does that mean?"

Deva grimaced. "Remember how we had to get naked before and you really kinda freaked out?"

I flattened my expression and glared at her. "Seriously?" Why was it always the naked stuff that we needed to do to get the magic to cooperate? Maybe the magic gods were just big pervs and liked watching us dance naked?

Carol and Beth tittered. "It's not so bad. You just eat Deva's brownie, and the dance draws magic from nature. I'll do the summoning, and the ghosts will come."

"While we're naked," I said.

"I figured we'd have to," Deva said. "I put robes in the car. As soon as they appear, you can slip a robe on." She went to the car, grabbed a pile of robes, and threw us each one.

Had she known this from the beginning? Ugh. She came so well prepared that she obviously suspected and they knew I wouldn't say no once we were all the way out here and trying to make it work. Manipulators, the lot of them. I huffed before grumbling, "Okay...I guess."

Five minutes later, Carols' phone played some Celtic melody into the darkened cemetery. At least the sun had fully gone down. No one should be able to see us from the road and as the harp and violin rose in pitch and intensity, I could feel the magic starting to do its thing.

My skin tingled. Carol had grabbed my magic. "Here." Deva handed me a small brownie. "Start dancing."

It was super awkward at first, but then, about thirty seconds into chewing the brownie, it kicked in. Thank heavens for that because I was about to cave and pull my robe back on.

It wasn't like being high, exactly. It was more like feeling powerful. I could sense my connection with nature, like a rope of gold, tying me to the earth, the trees, even the air around me. Nature didn't give a rat's behind about clothes so why should I?

My body danced without thought, my arms swaying over my head as I spun and stepped. The music carried me instead of me trying to follow the music. It was all there, I just had to let it take over.

Suddenly, ghosts surrounded us, dancing along with us. I squeaked and dropped to the ground, grabbing the robe Deva had laid out for me.

And just in time too. I stood up and faced a beautiful woman. Her face was long and angular, but not in a painful way, in a way that made her look like a model or at the very least someone who should be photographed. Even though she was in her misty ghost form I could see that her hair had been brown, a rich chestnut would have been my guess from the way there were subtle highlights throughout. Her eyes were probably green or blue and as she smiled it seemed like warmth was radiating out of her. "Hello," she said in a hollow voice. "You're Emma."

Oh, my gosh. I knew who she was. "You're Sarah. You're Daniel's wife." I whispered the end as my heart seized in my chest. Was she there to yell at me? To tell me to stay away from her husband.

She inclined her head once. "I am. And I'm so glad you summoned me."

I shrugged to get the robe more comfortable as I tied the belt around my waist. I tucked a lock of hair that had come free from my ponytail behind my ear. "I didn't exactly mean to, though I'm glad to meet you. He obviously loved you so much."

She smiled and ducked her head, like there was something she was trying to keep secret, something that was just for her and Daniel. When she looked back up it was just a normal smile before she said, "And I him. I wanted you to know I give you permission."

I gaped at her, not sure what to say. "Um, what?"

"I approve. Of your relationship." She stepped forward and pressed a feathery kiss to my cheek, that I hadn't realized I'd be able to feel. That was something I knew now. Ghosts could touch us. Then, she whispered, "He's been sad for so long, while I'm happy. I want us to both be happy."

Then, to my shock, she grabbed my shoulders and whirled me around as she said, "Nothing was an accident."

To face my mom and dad.

For a second, I just froze, then I crumpled to the ground. I tried to say something, anything, but all I actually did was start crying. Sitting there, feeling emotional, with my parents in front of me made me feel like a little girl again. I was a child wanting a hug from her parents, wanting them to tell me it would all be okay.

It was only when I heard the gasps from my friends as they realized why I'd fallen to the ground that I seemed to come back to myself. I was sitting in front of my parents. How many people hope and pray and beg for an opportunity like that and I was just sitting there?

I pushed to my feet and wiped the tears from my cheeks as I took a hesitant step toward them. They were crying too, if ghosts could really cry, and that nearly set me off all over again.

"Nothing was an accident," my mom said as she reached toward me. Unlike with Sarah, my mom's fingers didn't connect, they just floated right through my arm. She frowned and looked disappointed.

"What your mother is trying to say is all of our accidents weren't accidents," my dad said before pushing his glasses up on his nose. He takes a breath to say more but they flicker in and out, just like Thomas had done back at home.

"You're in danger. You and Daniel. That's what we need you to know. That's why we broke our rest," my mom said as she watched me. I looked so much like her, I hadn't realized it until I was standing in front of her, and it felt like I was looking in a mirror. Slightly distorted? Yes. But a mirror nonetheless, though I did have my dad's nose. It felt odd recognizing parts of myself in my parents, two people I'd missed beyond measure.

"The answers you seek, the way to protect yourself and Daniel, are buried on your lands," my dad added. His words were strained, as though he was trying to fight against something to get his point across. Was it the curse? The same one that stopped Thomas from telling us who was messing with him. As they both started to flicker even more, I realized that they looked like shadows created by a fire whose flames were sputtering and dying out. I wasn't ready for them to leave again. Not yet.

There was so much I wanted to say, wanted to ask, wanted to talk to them about, but I knew we didn't have time. Just like Thomas had disappeared, my parents would too, except hopefully they returned to their rest. "I love you. Henry loves you. I wish you could see the man he's become.

We miss you," I said, or tried to. My voice cut out at the end as tears choked me once more.

"We l-l-love you both—" my mom said before her voice gave out like a telephone line being cut.

"S-s-so pr-pr-proud." My dad's final words made the tears come once more. They both vanished, fading back into the ether, before I could say anything more, but I guess all the important stuff had been said. We loved each other. They were proud of us.

Oh, and I was in danger.

Again.

NINETEEN

Emma

MY PHONE BEEPED, once again when I was nearly asleep. I was exhausted. After having a very brief discussion warning Henry to be careful, I'd been even more tired. I'd almost told him about mom and dad, but he was speaking to his buddies in his game over his headset, so I figured I'd have to wait for a better time.

Then, I'd washed my face and braided my hair, and was snuggled in under a thick comforter with my fan blowing full blast. Almost nothing could've gotten me to look at my phone at that moment, but it was Daniel's ringtone. And, for Daniel, I'd make the effort to turn my head *slightly*.

So, I groaned and squinted at the screen.

I promise to be careful.

I smiled reading the text from him. We'd had a long conversation after the graveyard about what had happened. I'd told him everything. Even about his wife. We'd both sat together on my front steps, and he'd held my hand, his palm warm against mine. The thing was, it wasn't like we were both sad and suffering together, it was almost like we had felt this unexpected relief when it came to the people we lost. Our loved ones were okay, and they wanted us to be happy.

Still, their message to us couldn't be ignored. And that *wasn't* a relief. I knew there was trouble afoot, but the fact that we were in real danger, again, made me feel sick to my stomach.

Picking up my phone, I typed, letting my feelings out even if maybe I shouldn't have. **I'm still worried and scared. I can't help it. All I want to do is go to sleep, but I don't feel safe.**

Is there an officer still there?

I typed back. **No, there was some big issue with some local teens, and he had to go help.** I told him it was fine. What was I supposed to say? No. Sit out front. Ghosts had warned me that I was in trouble.

I stared at my phone, nibbling my bottom lip, but no reply came. Maybe I should've pretended to be strong. Or just said something badass-like. But it was too late now.

My fingers typed something to cover my tracks, but froze, then erased the words. Tried again. Still felt like an idiot and deleted the words.

I was scared. Maybe with Rick I always had to pretend to be tough, but I didn't want to make that mistake with Daniel. So, I left the message as it was and forced myself to put my phone down.

A while later, there was a soft knock on my bedroom door. "Come in," I called, expecting Henry.

To my shock, it was Daniel. "Hey," he said. "Henry let me in."

For a minute I just stared at him. He was wearing a thin, white t-shirt that hugged his big arms and big shoulders. He was wearing plaid pajama pants, and his hair was a little messy, as if he'd rolled right out of bed to see me. Actually, everything about him screamed a comfortable man who had just rolled out of bed, and it was strangely sexy.

I didn't know why he was here, but I was more than a little glad he was. Just having him in my room made me feel a strange mixture of nervousness and happiness. That was nice too.

Sitting up slowly, I smiled. "Uh, come in. Sit."

He sat on the side of the bed. "I couldn't sleep. I was worrying about you worrying."

This guy was so sweet it made me want to wrap him in a big hug.

Instead, I did what came instinctively to me. I scooted over and patted the spot I'd just vacated. "Sleep here."

"You sure?" he asked, smiling.

I nodded.

He kicked off his shoes and slid under the blankets with me. Then, glanced over at me, and ran his fingers through his auburn hair. "I should warn you, sometimes I snore a bit."

"I should warn you. I'm so tired that I'm going to pass out soon."

"Good," he said. "You sleep. I'll sleep. But keep in mind, the bear in me is going to know if there's an issue."

"Music to my ears," I said with a sigh as I scooted down and set my head on my pillow.

"Is it okay if I hold you a little?" He seemed nervous.

"Of course. I love to be cuddled while I sleep."

"Well, you know they call people cuddle *bears* for a reason."

I gave a tired laugh and rolled away from him, surprised my eyes were already fluttering shut. At any other time, on any other day, there was no way I could sleep with this hottie in my bed. I'd spend the whole night holding myself stiffly, scared to snort or fart, or whatever I did while I slept.

But today? I had zero shot of staying awake.

After a second, his arms went around my waist, and I sighed. He scooted a little closer, leaving a small amount of space between our bodies, but I could still feel the heat radiating off his body. It was comforting. I fell asleep quickly, and my sleep was like the dead.

For a while.

At some point, the dream started. I was a little girl standing on the beach outside of our house. My parents were smiling but sensed something was really important. My mom carried Henry on her hip and said something, but I wasn't sure what. My dad waved me over to follow him. We ducked behind the steps leading from our house to the beach, and I saw that my dad had dug a deep hole and that there was a metal container in the hole.

I couldn't hear what he was saying, but I knew he was telling me this box was really important. He started to bury it while I played with the bows on my purple dress, and he accidentally got some dirt on one of the white bows. I remember that really clearly. My mom couldn't get the stain out, and I got upset and never wore the dress.

This happened. It wasn't just a strange dream.

I woke with a jerk, as if I'd fallen from a high distance. Light drifted through the blinds of my window, and the clock flashed that it was seven in the morning. The dream... it'd felt so real. No, it *was* real. A memory.

Daniel's arm wrapped around me from behind, and I

turned to look back at him as he blinked rapidly. "Are you okay?" he asked.

His question brought it all into focus, and I felt my heart race.

"Yes, but I know where it is."

"Where what is?"

"What they were telling us about. The answer."

Daniel's eyes widened. "That's crazy, because... because I do, too."

"Then we better get going!" And then I smelled my own breath.

I clapped my hand over my mouth and tried to scoot out of the bed without blowing my morning breath in his face, but he jumped up and held out his hand to help me. I couldn't help it as I scooted over to get out of bed, with Daniel's assistance, my face was almost right in his crotch.

And they hid absolutely nothing of his morning wood.

A blush exploded across my face, and when I stood, I looked anywhere but down. Was that a natural morning erection or was it from snuggling close to me all night?

I didn't know, and since I wasn't about to ask, I'd just go with he was happy to see me.

"Um, you're welcome to the bathroom first," I said, nodding toward my en suite.

He grinned and stretched, *completely* unashamed of his morning situation. "Thanks."

Then the incorrigible man pressed a kiss to my cheek before sauntering into my bathroom.

Oh, my goodness. Morning wood, at *our* age.

TWENTY

Carol

I TOOK a deep breath and reached for my glove compartment. Inside, I had a lint brush. One thing about spending so much time with Beth was that pet hair got everywhere. Technically, I hadn't seen her this morning, but I still spotted hair on my clothes.

Rolling the lint brush over my dress, I smiled down at the pale blue dress with the little ice cream cones on it. The day I'd spotted this fabric, I'd known I had to snag it and make a dress. I'd made it in a fifties style, and complimented it with a hair band, tied to the side, and white pumps.

I smiled at myself in the mirror, smacked my bright red lips together, then put the brush away and headed out of my car. There were only two cars outside of the library this morning, which made sense because it was before opening hours.

As I walked along, the wind picked up, carrying with it a slight chill. I shivered and looked toward the library. It was a good-sized brick building with a huge, wild park area behind it. Tucked into one corner was a playground for the kids, but most of the library's lands had walking trails that weaved around the lake behind the library.

My gaze caught something red, and I froze. There was a small piece of torn fabric in the tree near one path. It was flapping in the breeze like a small flag. An old memory bubbled back to me of Bryan and me. He had worn a red shirt the day we had come here, and we'd taken that same path. Seventeen-year-old me had told him to catch me, and I'd taken off. He obliged, like he always did. All of the things that other guys found "quirky" about me, he just seemed to love.

I'd run as far as my legs could take me, and then he'd caught me in his big arms and swung me around. We'd ended up in some tall grass, and he'd kissed me. It wasn't my first kiss, but it was definitely my favorite one. When he'd pulled back, I'd stared up at him, combing my fingers through his hair. With the sky behind him, he'd looked like a painting of a beautiful man. Even now, I could picture him perfectly.

Except, what would he look like now as a man?

Tension raced through my body. No, I wouldn't think of that. Knowing him, he was living in some perfect, little cottage with a woman he adored and a few birds. He and I had both wanted birds rather than kids.

And that thought made my heart ache.

I turned away from the red fabric, squared my shoulders, and kept going toward the library. Memories of Bryan always crept up like that, like a spirit that was haunting me. It made me feel pathetic. Since Bryan, I'd been on easily a hundred dates and never felt that same spark, never felt that pull toward someone else, even when I tried, but I didn't want to think of him. Thinking of him just hurt.

Climbing the few steps that lead up to the door, I pulled one of the two big doors open, and I was immediately hit by the scent of old books. It was my second favorite scent, dwarfed only by the smell of new fabric. I grinned and walked in, flouncing a little because I loved the way it felt walking that way with my dress.

"Hey, Glynda," I called to our librarian. "Thanks for letting me in early!"

She smiled at me over her cup of coffee. Her feet were up on her desk, and she had a book in hand. "No problem. You've let me in the store early enough times."

I grinned back at her. It was true, Glynda loved my yarn almost as much as I did. She was even wearing a pretty green sweater that matched her eyes that was made from yarn from my store. I remembered her excitement when she came up to the counter to check out and had held it up next to her face, her eyes alight with excitement.

"Wish me luck!"

She chuckled as I walked past her desk.

I wanted to get my research done before I opened my fabric store. I didn't have to stay there today; my assistant was working. But I didn't want to be tied up here researching people long dead all day either.

I made a beeline for the local section and pulled out yearbooks from our parents' years at Mystic Hollow High, our years, and the years of people before and after us. Spinning with the yearbooks in my arms, I started singing a little song that makes me feel like a detective in an old show. I spread the books down on the table and grinned, before spreading out my skirts and plunking down in a chair.

Time to get to work!

I forced myself not to look out the window when I heard a bird chirping. Emma needed help figuring this whole thing out, and I was not going to let her down. Taking the first book off the top, I released a slow breath. I wasn't even sure what I was looking for but had a feeling I'd know it when I saw it.

It took a little while of thumbing through the pages before something stuck out to me. Taking a magnifying glass out of my purse, I laid out all the books on the pages in question and studied the images carefully, my heart racing. It was such a small thing, and yet, it felt significant. Emma's parents and Daniel's wife all had a pin on their lapels. It was an equal sign.

Weird. Maybe there was some math club. But I combed through that yearbook and found nothing.

I felt a little stupid obsessing about the symbol, but I had this strange feeling at the back of my neck that this was important. A clue connecting all of them. I jotted down the symbol on a piece of paper, and put a question mark next to it. Without any other ideas, I went back through my graduating year and looked to see if anyone had that pin on.

Another bird chirped and sat on the window outside the library. I gave it one longing look, then forced myself to keep looking at our yearbook. My eyes were beginning to hurt as I squinted at one person after another, running my gaze over them to see any sign of the symbol.

And then, I froze.

What the heck? Louisa was wearing the same pin and so was Jackson. That was a pretty big coincidence. But it also made me wonder if we were even on the right track. There's no way Jackson, the fast-talking brownie, was in on something sinister. Louisa? Yeah, that lady seemed like the type who went looking for trouble.

Still, this couldn't just be ignored.

"Hey, Glynda," I called.

After a minute, she appeared at the end of the shelves of books that I was seated by. "Yes?"

"Have you ever heard of a math club that's got an equal sign as their logo?" I asked.

She shook her head. "No, but there is one book over in the math section with an equal sign as the title. What a pain to file in the card catalog!"

Oh! That's officially a lead!

I jumped up. "Thanks, Glynda!"

Sure enough, I skimmed the titles of all the books about geometry and algebra and all that other number stuff I was terrible at. And there it was. A book with an equal sign.

I flipped it open and to my surprise found it was handwritten. Had nobody ever actually looked inside this thing?

Mystic Hollow needed more math geniuses, it seemed.

I took it back to my table and started reading. That crawling feeling along my skin was instantly back as I took in the words. This book had nothing to do with math, and everything to do with the supernatural world. It was all about shifters and humans being unequal. They wanted to find a way to be as powerful as the paranormals. This was a club where humans were trying to gain power. *Holy crap!*

It ended with information about a way to bind power from the "after" but it would require a powerful supernatural person on earth. It listed possibilities.

Karma was on the list. Double crap.

I thumbed through it again, reading more. It wasn't just humans involved in this whole thing though. The supernatural who took part in this club said they believed in equality, and they wanted to tell the school the truth. They wanted all restrictions to be removed and be able to live their lives out in the open, without hiding their special abilities.

What a disaster that would be! There was a reason we hid what we are from humans. One thing that history had shown is that humans desired power above all else and were willing to ignore ethics to get it and hurt those that had it.

I grabbed my phone and texted my girls pictures of these pages. Moving quickly, I grabbed the yearbook with Emma's parents in it, the equality book, and turned to check them out from Glynda.

But someone stood right behind me. Disappointment and anger warring in their eyes. I gasped and fear and dropped everything in my hands. "You?"

TWENTY-ONE

Emma

I couldn't hold my sneeze in any longer. I managed to roll away from Daniel and sneeze in the opposite direction, at least. A cloud of dirt flew up from the ground at the force of it and I was left sputtering and coughing afterward.

The crawlspace under my childhood home wasn't a place I'd ever imagined I'd be digging in, but here we were crawling like prisoners escaping from jail. And when I said crawl, I really meant, *crawl*. I was on my hands and knees, while Daniel was stuck practically shimmying his bulky form through the space. It highlighted the difference between our builds, and I wasn't mad about it. He was a bear, so I expected him to be big, and snuggling with him last night had only given me a taste of that, and seeing him now, working so hard, I wanted more.

Okay, maybe I should focus. Daniel was the one doing the digging and I was holding the light, but I was just as covered in dirt as he was. That meant I was putting in work too, right? How he was able to get enough leverage to actually dig under here when he couldn't even get on his hands and knees was a mystery, one I was happy to leave alone.

"Oh," Daniel said, startling me from openly staring at him. "Something is here."

We'd been digging for a while. My dream hadn't given a precise location for the box, just a general one, so we'd had to try a few different locations. There were about six new holes in the dirt under the area near the back porch steps.

It wasn't like my dream had drawn me a map. If it had that would have been much more helpful, but all I'd envision was the space under the house near the back steps.

I scooted over and held the light closer, and with only one hand, while helping Daniel dig with the other. In my head, I pretended it was fresh, clean sand rather than old, wet dirt that could be full of all manner of bugs and spiders.

Eww.

We worked in silence for a while, the two of us moving load after load of sand away from our target. After another five minutes, Daniel shifted position. "It's a sizable box," he said. "I have to get underneath it."

"Underneath it? You mean dig further down?" I asked, confused.

"No, just get to the one end so I can pull it out." That made a lot more sense.

It only took him another minute in this position, and a metal box finally popped up and out of the ground. He grabbed it and began working his way toward the exit. Shimmy, pull, shimmy, pull, until he was able to back all the way out of the crawl space.

I followed gingerly, trying not to blind Daniel as I used the light to make sure I didn't move over or squish any of the creepy-crawlies I kept imagining. Luckily for my sanity, they all seemed to be in my head, and we escaped the crawl space largely unharmed. I sent a silent thank you to all the bugs for staying out of our way and not terrifying me the way they could have.

Once I was out, I pushed up so I could stand, and realized how filthy we were. Some of the dirt came off easily, but I definitely needed a change of clothes, and my shoes were caked with mud. Urgh. I knew I should have taken the time to dig for my crappy pair of sneakers. Now these were probably ruined.

As much as I wanted to open that box *right now*, first I had to change. I knew I hadn't seen any bugs, but I couldn't shake the sensation of being dirty and possibly having bugs on me as a result. Nope. Couldn't handle it. "I'll be right back," I muttered.

"Actually, before I clean up, I'm going to run to my place and get the box under my house."

"Do you need help?" I asked, feeling bad abandoning Daniel to find his own box.

It was like he could see how much I was itching to get clean again because he just shook his head and waved me off as he said, "You go change and clean up. I'll be back soon."

I nodded. "Okay. I'll try to wait for you to get back."

Chuckling, like he knew how much it would take for me to wait for him to return, Daniel left, and I hurried upstairs. A quick glance in the mirror showed a big smear of mud in my hair.

Dang.

So, I had to shower again, meaning by the time I got out, Beth, Deva, Henry, and Alice had arrived. Still no Daniel yet though. I'd tried to take a quick shower. Honest. It just took more effort to get caked in mud out of my hair than I thought, and then to feel clean again afterward.

"Hey," I called into the kitchen as I toweled my hair. The box sat, ignored, on the coffee table. It called to me, seemingly almost literally, though of course that was just in my head. My hands itched to pull at the top to try and open it.

Deva walked out with a pink box that had to contain goodies and handed it right over. I pulled out a big chocolate donut and took a huge bite while I stared at the box. "I want to open it," I said around the donut.

Deva chuckled. "What's stopping you?"

Everyone sat as I explained, and Beth handed me freshly brewed coffee. The aroma seemed to call to my very soul as I took a deep breath. "You're a bunch of saints." I took a scalding sip, not caring that I burnt my tongue a bit, then carried on. "Well, we had this dream at the exact same time. My parents told me this box was here and Daniel's ex-wife told him his was under their house. It seems appropriate that we open them at the same..." I trailed off when I heard the distant sound of a car door. "Oh, he's back." I had to fight the urge to jump up from my seat and go to the front door to wait like an anxious puppy. I could wait calmly with my coffee like a sensible person.

Sure enough, a minute later, Daniel came hurrying through the door with his hair still wet. "Sorry it took so long," he said breathlessly. "I took a quick shower after traipsing around under the houses."

"It's okay." Beth got up so Daniel could join me on the couch and went to get him a cup of coffee, which I was grateful for since I was exhausted from this morning, and I hadn't even been the one doing the digging. My hip and back were more than a little irritated from the position I'd been stuck in this morning. He put his box beside mine and accepted a coffee from Beth and donuts from Deva.

"Shall we?" I asked Daniel once he had a mouthful of deep-fried goodness and a swig of caffeine.

"Just be ready," Deva said with a smile. "I'm having someone drop off lunch for us in a few minutes."

"Yay!" I grinned.

We lifted the lids on the metal boxes at the same time. They both squeaked and squealed in unison and made a sucking sound when they finally released as though they had been hermetically sealed or something. We all leaned forward to see the contents. I was honestly surprised the boxes had opened so easily and hadn't been locked or something. I mean sure, the age and elements made them difficult to open but if someone had known where these were then once they got the box, they would have easily been able to open them. Once I saw what was inside the seal that we seemed to break made more sense. It had to have been some kind of magic or spell. Paper buried in a metal box wouldn't have survived the years otherwise, and the contents still looked like they were in pretty good shape.

"Journals?" Deva asked. "Is that it?" Her brow was furrowed as she looked at the contents, and I was sure she was wondering the same thing I was, why would my parents and Daniel's wife go to such lengths to protect and hide some journals.

Daniel and I grabbed the journals, a handful at a time and handed them out to our friends. Everyone dug in. Belatedly, I looked around and furrowed my brow. I'd been so focused on the box I hadn't realized Carol wasn't right along with us here. "Where's Carol?"

Deva shrugged. "She said something about going to the library." She pulled out her phone to call her, but I got totally engrossed in the journals. "Ohh," Beth said. "I found enchantments." My gaze skimmed over the pages in front of me and I wasn't sure what I was seeing at first but to me they looked like spells of some kind. Protection maybe? Divination possibly? There were pages and pages of them, each with a slightly different heading to the point that I wasn't sure if it was just drafts of the same spell or different spells completely.

Daniel's journals stopped the show. "I can't believe it," he whispered.

Any interest I had in figuring out what was in my journals took a pause at his tone. "What?" I asked, leaning over to try to read his book. The handwriting was definitely feminine so probably his wife's, but it was also squished and extra curly to the point that I was having a hard time reading it.

Finally, Daniel said, "My wife was researching a spell she believed your parents had performed on you." He met my gaze. "One to open you up to magic."

Open me up to magic? What the hell? What did my parents even know about magic? And could you really open a human up to magic? My head was spinning with questions, and I had no idea how I was going to find any answers.

The doorbell rang.

"That'd be lunch," Deva said.

But suddenly, I wasn't hungry.

TWENTY-TWO

Emma

"Did you ever get a call back from Carol?" Beth asked, her voice tinged with concern. I looked up from my journal and found Beth staring at her own phone as though she was mentally willing Carol to call her.

Deva looked up from what she was reading and blinked slowly. Once she seemed to be back with us, and not lost in the world these journals were talking about, she reached out and grabbed her phone. The screen came to life but there were no missed calls or notifications, just a photo of cake. The woman knew how to choose her lock screens, I'd give her that. "Oh, geez, no. And it's almost dinner time. We've been sitting here reading this stuff most of the day."

I understood her owlish blinking. My brain was fuzzy from being so engrossed in the journals. And now that I wasn't thinking about the words on the page, my stomach growled, and I really needed a glass of Henry's lemonade. He really did make some of the best lemonade I'd ever had. My brain must have been mush if I was thinking more about lemonade than where Carol had run off to.

"I'll try to get her again," Beth said. She stood and walked into the kitchen with her cell as we turned back to the journals. I slowly ate from the lunch Deva had dropped off hours ago, while studying the journal. There was just so much information in them to absorb. They had documented everything, every trial, every mistake, everything they could get their hands on. It still wasn't clear what exactly they were trying to accomplish though. It was like they thought even writing it down would get them in trouble.

"So, your parents thought someone was watching you?" Daniel asked, studying me with those jade eyes of his.

I nodded. The thought creeped me out. I'd just been a little girl at the time of the entry that told us what they suspected. "They were worried I'd been marked by the paranormal community, but they didn't know or understand why." I pointed to a line in one of the journals. "They worried that if they couldn't perform this spell, I'd end up dead, but they never said what the spell was." I flipped to the end. "The journals end with the suggestion that something worked, and something went wrong. And that my whole family might have been in danger."

He nodded as though that helped him understand his own reading, or maybe he just understood my frustration. "My wife's journals start years later. She was pulled into the organization, or club or whatever it was, by someone she refers to as Z. As the journals progress, it's clear she goes down the same path as your parents."

I wanted to scream. But there wasn't much we could do now to warn Sarah. They were so eager for the barriers to come down between humans and supernatural beings that Sarah had got herself in deep with someone dangerous. I hated that Daniel had lost his wife and I hated even more that it hadn't just been a tragic accident, that someone had intentionally snuffed out the warmth of her from the world.

"These end with..." Daniel turned pages to the end, his fingertips grazing the paper carefully until he found what he's looking for. "In the last entry it says she suspects that what happened to Emma's parents was Z's fault and now she's worried she's in danger, too. It says she told Thomas!" Daniel looked at me in surprise, then read more. "Said he figured it out, so she told him the truth."

I sighed. "We're going to get to the bottom of this and stop all this nonsense. Once and for all." I just didn't know how...yet.

Daniel

My chest was aching like I was being stabbed over and over again. Going through all this stuff with Sarah, reading her handwriting... it was like she'd just died a few days or weeks ago. Not years. I could almost smell her perfume on the pages as well, like this time capsule was trying to torture me. It was even worse since I was sitting right next to Emma.

My emotions were all tangled now, even though Sarah had given us her blessing I felt strange about everything. It wasn't that I didn't want Emma, I very much did, but with all this stuff about Sarah being brought back up I felt like I was reliving losing her all over again.

How was it possible that I'd never known all these things about my wife? She was my wife, and she was keeping a secret this big from me? I couldn't stop myself from feeling a bit betrayed. I knew she didn't mean anything by it, but it still hurt. Had she not trusted me enough to talk about this? Did she think I was too much of a stickler for the rules to tell me? Or was she worried this would draw me back to Emma?

To top it off, the thought of foul play had never even crossed my mind. Now, the knowledge that she could have been murdered sent chills through me. I was a cop, I should have looked into it more, should have realized that there was something off about the accident. Shoulda, woulda, coulda...

As my therapist would say, I was should-ing on myself again. The past is the past and we react the best way we can in the moment. I had to believe that, or I would start questioning everything.

Between Sarah being murdered and me not knowing about this obsession of hers I was beginning to wonder what else I didn't know?

My phone pinged with a text. I slipped it from my pocket, worried that it might be something to do with Nathan again. Fortunately, it was just Joel letting me know my truck was finally ready. It would be a shame to see the fancy green truck I'd been driving around go, but I loved *my* truck and all the memories she contained, including all the scratches and dings, which this loaner didn't have. The thing practically looked brand new.

"Should I have dinner delivered?" Deva asked, yawning. "It's getting late."

Emma looked like she was about to answer when Beth walked in. I could sense that she was worried and when she spoke, I understood why. "Guys, I can't get a hold of Carol. I know she can be a little absent-minded at times, but with everything going on, I think it's better to be safe than sorry. Let's go see if we can find her. She said she was going to the library, right?"

I watched as Deva nodded. "She's probably just fallen down a rabbit hole of books or something." Deva's words may have been reassuring, but I could see she was just as worried as Beth.

"Should I be looking into this?" I asked.

Deva gave me a smile. "Honestly, as reliable as Carol can be sometimes, she once showed up to dinner three hours late, because she had started making a dress and forgot we had plans. Chances are, this is nothing. It just never hurts to be careful."

Okay, as much as the protective bear inside of me seemed tense, these ladies knew their friend better than I did. Besides, there was already a lot going on.

I stood and smiled at Emma, who looked like the world rested on her shoulders. I knew all three of them were worried, but I also knew I'd be more helpful to them, and to whatever it was that we were trying to figure out if I had my own truck. The loaner was nice, but I felt like I had to drive like a grandpa, so I didn't damage it. I wasn't exactly a reckless driver having been a cop but the fact that it wasn't mine made me extra cautious. "I'll meet you guys there. My truck is finally ready."

Instinctually, I went to Emma and pressed a light kiss on her cheek.

Some of the weight I'd sensed hanging on her lessened, and she gave me one of those little smiles that made my heart ache. "You be careful out there."

"You too," I told her. I wanted to say more, but Deva and Beth were grinning at me.

Yup, we could talk later. I might not be afraid of PDA, but I didn't like having an audience either.

I glanced down at the journals, where the pages had flipped to rest, there was a weird symbol of an equal sign.

Maybe I'd seen it before and not put it together. I mean it was just an equal sign. Anyone looking at it out of context would just assume some weird club or math obsession.

There was something twisting in my gut though, something that told me this wasn't just going to go away by itself. Something majorly sinister had been brewing in this town for a very long time.

TWENTY-THREE

Emma

"YOU GUYS GETTING INTO TROUBLE AGAIN?" Henry asked, munching his favorite sandwich, white bread, and cheddar cheese.

I sighed. "Yeah, a little. These are old journals from mom and dad. It looks like they got into some trouble." I hesitated. "And that maybe their deaths weren't an accident."

Henry stopped chewing. "What do you mean?"

"I'm still figuring it out," I rushed out. "But it's possible the car accident we were in, and the one that Thomas and Sarah were in, weren't accidents. That someone caused them and killed them on purpose."

"I can't see mom and dad getting into that kind of trouble."

I would have agreed with him if I hadn't read the journals myself or had them talk to me. "I recently spoke with their ghosts."

He lifted a brow. "They don't usually talk."

My jaw dropped open. "You've really seen them before? I wasn't sure..."

He hesitated, then shook his head. "Not exactly. But... I don't know how to explain it. My brain works differently than other people's. Whenever I tried to explain it, people acted like it was my autism, so I stopped trying. But I described it to Alice, and she said it seemed like my parents wrapped their presence around me at important moments in my life. I'm even pretty sure they did it for you too."

I tried not to react, to ignore the way my eyes stung. Henry would get stressed if I did and maybe stop talking. So, I turned to my friends. "Have you ever heard of humans who could sense or see ghosts?"

Beth shook her head, but then Deva spoke. "There are humans with supernaturals in their blood lines, so they're sensitive to those kinds of things. They're usually people who excel at art, or math, or science. It seems to come easily to them, but it has to do with their bloodline. There are even humans who have a greater ability to sense auras, ghosts, etc. But they always have some splash of magic in their blood. Maybe someone in your family line was magical?"

That was hard for me to believe.

"I never showed any unique abilities." I gave a tired laugh. "And everything I did was always hard. Nothing ever came easily."

Beth smiled. "You were always good with people. They kind of seemed drawn to you."

I laughed again. "I don't think so."

"Do you mind if I read their journals?" Henry asked. "Maybe I can figure out something you missed."

"Go for it!"

He nodded, but I knew he'd have to finish his sandwich

and wash his hands before touching the journals. It was one of the things that were important to him.

"Just be careful," I said, grabbing my purse.

"Because of the would-be murderer?"

I smiled. "Yeah." That *was* something I'd warned him about when he'd come in for a snack earlier.

"Okay. I've pretty much decided to be careful since you got back."

Man, that was hard to hear him say.

"Sorry to have brought so much trouble into your life," I said and felt a wave of guilt.

"Having you here in person, rather than just on the video chats, more than makes up for all the trouble. Besides, I'm pretty sure I'd have been murdered by sirens if you hadn't showed up."

He had a point.

"Besides, I'm having some gamer friends over later."

I was a little surprised. "Really?"

He shrugged. "Yeah. They're the same group I always play with. I've met all of them except one up until now. But tonight, one guy had the awesome idea to bring all our computers together and have an epic LAN party, so I'm excited for that. As long as they don't touch my setup."

"I guess I'll be coming home to a party," I said. "Try not to let it get too wild."

He seemed to take me seriously. "Not to worry. We have headsets. We shouldn't bother the neighbors."

It took everything in me not to laugh. LAN parties I could handle a lot more than him gambling at vampire clubs. He could have a computer party here every night from now on, for all I cared.

I gave him a quick half-hug, and my friends and I went outside. There was still no officer outside. Apparently, the local teens had had a big party on a cliff, and some kids had gotten seriously hurt. A lot of the kids had taken off. Some had gotten lost in the woods. It was an all-hands on deck kind of situation. And because I figured we were okay with Daniel, I'd just accepted it.

Now I kind of wished there was someone to watch Henry. But there wasn't much I could do about that now.

Releasing a slow breath, I kept walking to my car. Henry was smart and fully capable of keeping himself safe. He'd been fine all these years without me here, so I wasn't going to start babying him now.

The three of us loaded into my car and headed for the library. In my mind, I kept going through the most logical reasons that Carol hadn't shown up and hadn't answered her phone. Deva was right. I loved Carol, but she could be a bit absentminded. It was one of the things I loved most about her. I remember one time in high school she missed a test because she'd thought she'd seen a kitten in a bush. She ended up going on a big search for the thing and ended up finding nothing. She swore to our teacher that a kitten had needed her, and the teacher had just sighed and let her retake the test after school. Or it could be a bird, I knew she got really excited when she saw an unusual one and almost everything else would go out the window.

And besides, I think all of us would turn off our phones in the library. It could be a simple mistake.

Or something scary and dangerous.

But I refused to think about that. Carol was one of my best friends. She was fine. The ghosts had said Daniel and I were in trouble, not Carol.

Still, my heart was racing as we got closer to the library.

"She's okay." Deva's voice shook a little.

"She better be, or Karma is going to destroy someone," I said.

"She might not even be here," Beth said, her voice a little too high. "Maybe she went home and took a nap. Or she got busy with a customer."

Maybe...

We pulled into the library parking lot. It was fairly empty, but that wasn't exactly surprising given that the local library wasn't exactly a hot spot for the locals.

"Look." I nodded toward the far end of the lot. "Her car is here." Carol liked to park far away to help get her steps in. She loved getting that little buzz from her tracker that told her she'd hit her goal for the day.

"Maybe she got caught up doing something and her phone died," Beth suggested.

But Deva shook her head. "No, her phone was ringing. It's not off."

"Maybe just on silent?" I asked.

"Maybe," Deva said, but it felt like she was saying *no*.

We all climbed out of my car and headed for the big library doors. Normally, I liked this place. It felt soothing, almost like Beth or Carol's shops. Looking back at my high school years, I'd probably spent too many nights and weekends here, cramming for tests.

And maybe diving into every book I could get my hands on.

But as we walked up, it didn't feel soothing. It felt way too empty. Yeah, this wasn't a popular hang out, but people did go here. Right now, it looked...lifeless.

My nerves were jumping as I climbed up the steps to the library.

When we got to the front door, it was locked and everything inside was dark and quiet. "It's the middle of the afternoon." I peered through the window beside the door. "Why is it closed?"

"Anytime Glynda has to close up shop, her sister Glenna comes," Deva said. "And then there are volunteers. I've never seen these doors closed."

She was right.

"Hang on." Beth cracked her knuckles, rolled her head, then grabbed the handle. She narrowed her eyes, and a few seconds later, the door clicked. "Ha."

"Good going," I praised. We moved carefully into the library, looking for any signs of danger. If it weren't for being worried about Carol, we would've waited on Daniel. But there wasn't any time to wait if our friend was in trouble.

Creeping forward, we gasped almost as one when we spotted Glynda in her chair, draped back with her head lolling and arms flopped to the sides. My stomach flipped. Glynda wasn't that much older than us. She wouldn't have just died in her chair before opening up this morning...

No, she couldn't be dead. I wouldn't believe it.

I hurried to her side and pulled her arms in front of her, crossing them to be more comfortable. Then, I pressed my fingers against her neck. I had no idea how to feel for a pulse, but right away I felt a steady thump, thump against my fingertips. "She's alive."

"Thank goodness!" Beth said, and I could hear unshed tears in her voice.

"Glynda?" I said. "Glynda!" I repeated a little louder.

She didn't react. Not even a flicker of her eyelids.

I shook her shoulder, and she started to slump forward until I straightened her back up again, then frowned at the others. "Something about this isn't right."

Deva picked up Glynda's teacup and sniffed, while

studying the liquid. "That's a sleeping brew. Heavily hidden with lavender. It's an old trick."

"Why would anyone give her a sleeping brew?"

Deva frowned. "For trouble."

Darn it. She was right.

Quietly, but hurrying, we continued around the library, searching for Carol. We found a table with yearbooks spread across it, and a bright yellow handbag with a knitted image of a bird on it. We instantly knew that Carol had been working here. And yet, nothing was suspicious. It was just as if she was somewhere in the library, searching for more books.

So, we kept going through the library. Nothing was out of place until we came to the math section. There, a whole shelf of books had been thrown all over the floor, as if there was a struggle. I heard Beth gasp behind me, and heart thumping, I moved through the books. There wasn't any blood, nor anything else that said Beth was here. Except...

I knelt down. Two books were mixed in with all the math ones, but they looked more specifically placed rather than knocked down in a struggle. They were open, and definitely not math books.

"Yearbooks." I bent over and looked at them. "Open to our senior class and my parents' senior class." I turned and looked at Deva and Beth. "This makes no sense."

The ladies bent over the book and squinted.

"Do you see any reason it'd be open on this?" I asked.

"No," Deva said as Beth shook her head.

Beth tore something in her purse and handed me two scraps of paper that I used to book the pages. Then, I closed them and pulled them into my arms, pressing them against my chest.

Finally, my gaze met Deva's. "Do you think there was a struggle here?"

Deva's mouth curled into a frown. "Given that she was here to look at these books, the librarian was drugged, Carol's car is here, and yet she's nowhere to be found. Yeah, I think there was a struggle here. And I think Carol is in trouble."

That's what my instincts were screaming, and I hated it.

Dread and fear filled me. Something was very wrong, and Carol was missing.

TWENTY-FOUR

Daniel

I WALKED UP to the body shop with my hands in my pockets. I wanted to hurry over to the library, but I also didn't want to be a jerk and make Sheriff Danvers come hunt his truck down. So, I'd dropped it off a couple of blocks away at the police station, then hurried to get my truck. Even though it was a chilly evening, and my bear liked the chill normally, I wasn't enjoying the fresh air.

Not when my Emma and her friends were potentially walking into a dangerous situation.

The more I thought about it since leaving her house, the angrier I got with myself. I'd been so thrown off from reading the journals Sarah had written, it was like my cop instincts had flipped off. Yet the fresh air had brought me back to reality. Someone wanted to hurt Emma. Her friend wasn't answering her phone. Maybe Carol was fine, but I sure as hell should be with Emma, making sure.

I could hear the noise of the mechanic's shop before I

saw the big letters on the raggedy brick building. This was one of three shops in town, and definitely the one I liked best. Joel ran it, and he was always the type to get straight to the point and not charge for pointless stuff.

I just hoped Joel wasn't too busy and I could just get my truck and go.

But I had no such luck. The sound of something electrical stopped, and I could suddenly hear that some lady was inside the bay screaming at him. Not the, I need a cop's help, kind of screaming. More like, I wanted a whisper of cinnamon on my obnoxious drink and got a dollop of it.

Sigh.

"She's pretty ticked off."

I whirled to find Jackson, a half-brownie who nobody ever wanted to run into, off to the side of the garage. He had to have just walked around the building. Damn brownies. They were so sneaky at times. "What's up, Jackson?" I asked.

He shrugged. "I've been waiting to pick up my car, but Joel is dealing with..." He motioned toward the yelling woman. "Louisa."

Oh, that's who that was. "Ugh," I muttered. I'd worked with Louisa at the station. She was in the animal control department, which was technically under the sheriff department's purview.

She was not a pleasant woman. I'd wondered several times over the years if she really should be in charge of animals, but if I'd moved her out of that department, I would've had to deal with her on a regular basis. My patience had its limits, and since we didn't have a lot of stray animals or ones that needed rescuing, I left her where she was.

"This is going to take longer than I thought."

"Nah, Joel is pretty good at shutting down that kind of stuff."

I glanced back at Jackson. He was usually so chatty that it was actually weird for him to be so concise. "You okay?"

"Yeah," he blushed, his too-long hair falling over his forehead. "Actually, I met a lady a few days ago. You know Daisy, who runs the flower shop?"

I nodded, remembering a very quiet woman with short grey hair who always seemed to be hiding behind one plant or another. In high school, she hadn't been much different. Quiet, terribly shy, and only really comfortable when she seemed to be working with plants.

"I asked her on a date. And, well, we've been inseparable ever since." He looked at the shop with a frown. "Until today. I'm actually eager to get back to her."

Man, I wasn't exactly a romantic, but the thought of those two together actually made me smile. Jackson could be a bit annoying, but every pot had its lid. Maybe Daisy was his lid... or pot. Whatever. Maybe I wasn't the only one finding a new love at my crotchety old age.

I almost laughed to myself. I think I had to be eighty before I could comfortably call myself crotchety. But then, I really wanted to deserve the description. I'd sit at the edge of my lands and shake my fist at the young wolves. Yell at them to stay off my territory. Tell them how easy they had it. You know, all the fun stuff.

Well, maybe not if I had Emma back at the cabin waiting for me.

Louisa was still going on about her car taking so long and didn't seem to be stopping. I pulled my hands out of my pockets and steeled myself. It looked like I wouldn't be able to just wait until she was done.

"Well, I better face the music."

Jackson laughed. "May the force be with you."

He was nerdy too? Man, I actually kind of liked this guy when he wasn't just blathering.

I walked around to the back of the shop where the yelling was coming from, going through different scenarios that could get me in and out as fast as possible. I didn't want to get anywhere near a screeching Louisa, but I was already late meeting Emma at the library. And I had a horrible feeling that something was about to happen.

Joel shrugged when Louisa looked away to peer at her car, then she started yelling about a grease smudge on the hood. He shot me an apologetic look, but then when she looked at him again, his face morphed into one of innocence and worry. "Let me buff that out," he said. "And you can be on your way."

I was pretty sure Joel wasn't getting out from under Louisa's thumb for a while yet, so I wandered toward the back part of the bay where my truck was sitting, hopefully, ready to go. Joel usually had the vehicles that were finished in the lot behind his shop, but he must have been too busy to drive it out there yet. I just hoped when he called me to tell me it was ready, it wasn't like, "it'll be ready by the time you get here."

But sure enough, my truck was looking better than she'd looked in years. He'd cleaned up everything, had it washed, and even had those little papers on the floors, to protect the mats from grease. My baby was ready to go!

And since I'd already paid, I knew I could grab my keys, give him a wave, and he'd be relieved not to have another customer waiting while he was screeched at. It was one of the many benefits of a small town, that I'd been to this shop enough to know what to do.

A box on the wall held the customers keys. Joel locked it

at night to prevent thefts, but it sat open all day. Walking over to it, I snatched my keys from one of the hooks and turned back toward my friend. But before I opened my mouth to interrupt the furious Louisa, something caught my eye.

In a toolbox on the ground, just casually thrown to the side, was a pin. An equal sign the exact color and style of the one I'd seen in Sarah's journal.

The *exact* one.

Today.

There was no way this didn't mean something. I just hoped it didn't mean something bad.

I turned slowly toward Joel. What did he have to do with my wife?

TWENTY-FIVE

Emma

"Hey, you guys," I said in a hushed voice. We'd searched the entire library again, and Beth and Deva were using their magic to try to sense anything that might give us a clue where to go next or what to check. The whole thing came up empty though, as though someone had cleansed the entire library and made it a big blank spot.

I'd run out of things to try and had picked up the year-book that contained what I was sure would be my parents' beaming faces somewhere on this page. All of them looked so hopeful and innocent. It was hard to believe what my parents had coming. Two kids, a strange secret, and a horrible accident that wasn't an accident that brought about their untimely demise.

My gaze scanned over the black and white photos of each member of their graduating class until I found the first person I was interested in, my dad Anthony Foxx right, and then my mom, Elizabeth Nobleman. What I hadn't expected was what I saw next to her. Joel Northman.

"Holy crap," I breathed. "Look!"

"What?" Deva took the book and Beth peered over her shoulder. Both of them looked unimpressed. I knew the supernatural was common, but I hadn't expected Joel to be part of that. As far as I'd known he was human. But then there had been a lot I hadn't known.

"It's Joel." I pointed to his picture. His hair was perfectly combed back, and he wore a polo of some kind with the collar perfectly folded. "And he doesn't look a day over twenty here."

They looked at me blankly. "Okay?"

"Guys..." I furrowed my brow. Why weren't they seeing this? "*We* went to high school with Joel. Why is he in my parents' yearbook looking exactly the same?"

Deva's jaw dropped and Beth's eyes went wide. "Oh, my gosh," Deva breathed while Beth's jaw just dropped open. It was rare for her to be lost for words in a moment like this.

"Why would you go through high school twice?" Deva muttered as though the concept was horrific. "Most of the supernaturals around here have ways of making it so the humans don't realize they aren't aging at the same rate. But it isn't something they do that impacts the minds of super-naturals. And we don't just choose to go back to our years where we're young, in school, and under the thumbs of parents and teachers. Most supernaturals look between twenty and thirty for most of their lives... not seventeen. None of it makes sense"

"There had to be a reason. He wouldn't just do it because he missed taking classes or something," I said, knowing deep inside myself that this was going to all come together in a way none of us expected. All of this had to be connected though, it was too weird for it not to be.

"Maybe he just really loved math or something," Beth

added, grinning a little. Sure, now wasn't the best time for jokes, but if we didn't laugh sometimes, we'd all go crazy.

They switched volumes with me and poured over the photo of him in our yearbook. His hair was shaggier, and he was just wearing a t-shirt, but there was no mistaking that it was him. The more I stared at the local mechanic though, the more something else kept bothering me but I wasn't sure what it was... Until it hit me.

"Oh..." I stared at my friends. A cold chill raced over my skin and my body broke out in goosebumps. "Really focus on what you know Joel looks like now," I said. "I mean, *think hard.* Not what he's wearing, but his face."

A few seconds later, they caught up to me. "He hasn't changed since this picture in the yearbook with your parents in it," Beth said.

"So, this isn't one of those creeps who try to look younger to play football or something," Deva said with a frown.

"And, as far as you know, he's human?" I asked, just making sure.

They both nodded.

"The shifters would smell that he wasn't human," Beth said, slowly.

"And all us witches would sense that something was off," Deva added.

"You know all the paranormals in town?" I asked.

Again, they both nodded.

"Basically, we'd know if he was a supernatural... or should know." Deva looked even more upset. "If in a town like Mystic Hollow, he hid what he was, it was for a bad reason. I'm sure of it."

"Do you think that's why Carol is gone?" Beth's voice

was barely louder than a whisper. "Did she figure this out, and he came for her?"

I felt sick. "It's definitely possible."

Deva tossed the book onto the table. It hit the laminated surface with a smack and the pages all fluffed up before settling again. She turned with Beth and I hot on her heels. "We've got to get to the body shop and get to the bottom of this!" she called. She didn't need to be loud since we were right there, and it seemed we all had the same thought. I for one was willing to bet that wherever Carol was, Joel would be with her. I just hoped we weren't too late.

I also hoped that the sleeping potion wasn't too much for Glynda since she was still out like a light when we left. Beth made sure to lock back up, since we didn't want anyone accidentally hurting Glynda or causing any damage to the library. It was probably best to keep everything secure. Plus, it might slow Joel down if he went back there.

We got back into the car and there were only gray streaks left in the sky from the setting sun.

"That took too long," I said.

They both nodded, and the air got thick with tension.

I sent a quick text to Daniel letting him know what we'd found out, then shifted the car into drive. I wasn't usually a fast driver, but with Carol missing, and all signs pointing that Joel was involved, I was going to tap into my reckless teen days.

Thank goodness for small towns. The library was only about a two-minute drive from the body shop. If we'd cut through a side street, and across a couple people's back-yards, we probably could've run faster. Being without speedy transportation wasn't what I wanted though, not when I saw what waited for us.

As soon as we pulled into the body shop parking lot, I

knew that Joel knew someone was on to him. Maybe he just thought it was Carol or maybe he was starting to freak out. Either way, the whole place was shut down and dark. Joel never closed during the day. He hardly ever closed. Period. In a small town he was one of the few mechanics, which meant being available at odd hours, and being willing to work when everyone else had already gone home.

There were only a few places that constantly had some kind of light on, and Joel's shop was one of them. Even if he was gone for the day there was normally a light on in the parking lot. Tonight though, there was nothing. The moon, thankfully, was bright enough that we didn't need it. That didn't make it any less weird though.

"This is as unsettling as the library was," I whispered. The metal roll doors were all down and I didn't need to try the handle on the door to the waiting area and business side of the shop to know it was locked.

We got out and looked around cautiously. One of the big bay doors hadn't closed all the way so there were a couple inches open at the bottom. I debated for a moment between stealth and getting into the shop and decided that getting in was more important. As I hooked my fingers under the door and pulled, it gave a little before stopping. The gears and chains that moved the door weren't exactly quiet and made me wince at the noise. There was no way around it though, not if we wanted to get inside. "I think we can squeeze under there," I said quietly.

"Let's make sure nobody's in there." Deva stood on her tiptoes and peered inside through the tiny window or vent that was in the roll door while Beth put her hand on the building.

"I think someone is," Beth said. "But I don't feel any current threat. Just sadness and anger. Residual."

"Good." I got down on my hands and shimmied under the door, using my body to push it as far up as it could go. I had to squeeze one boob underneath and then the other. My back protested the movement sharply and my neck twinged like my whole body was threatening me, but I ignored the pain.

Once I was through, I pushed carefully to my feet, trying not to anger my back any further, but then I did something stupid and pulled on the door, forcing it a little higher so Deva and Beth could get underneath. When I straightened up my back said I'd be paying for that mistake later.

When the girls joined me, we looked around in shock. The lights were off but there was enough ambient light that came in through the vents and the windows in the office to show a total mess.

Tools were strewn everywhere, and a couple of tool-boxes turned over. And worse, many of them had been spat-tered with blood. There were smears of oil on the walls as though someone had been trying to do a Jackson Pollock with oil and blood. What I found most concerning was the stench of gasoline. Obviously, it would smell a little like that, it was an auto shop after all, but this was too strong. It was like an entire gas can had been tipped over and it was soaking the floor somewhere, only I didn't see where. What-ever had happened here, it wasn't good.

"Do you guys smell that?" I asked as I brought the edge of my t-shirt up to my nose to try and block some of it out.

They both nodded, their faces grim. None of us were getting good vibes from this place or what had happened before we got here.

"Look," Deva said. "She pointed to the side of a car. "Isn't that Louisa's car?"

I had no idea, but Beth said she thought it was. All I could focus on was the huge claw marks in the passenger door.

Like bear claws.

"Daniel was definitely involved," I said.

"Do you think Louisa is here?" Beth said, her voice soft and frightened.

"If she is, Joel better hope he's not, or I'm going to unleash Karma on his ass," I growled.

"Check the office," Deva said, nodding in one direction. We all rushed toward the door on the far side of the bay.

It was locked, but Beth did her thing. Come to think of it, we probably should have had her do that to the office door outside. That would have saved us struggling underneath a huge metal roll door.

The second the door was thrown open, we all froze. Inside, thrown on the floor, was Carol. Tied up. But with her eyes open and frightened.

"Oh, thank goodness," I breathed. We rushed in and untied Carol, who seemed largely unhurt. There was a graze on her forehead and her hair was all messed up like she'd been thrown about a bit or just had a roll in the hay. My biggest concern was actually what was in her mouth.

"Are you okay?" I cried as I pulled the dirty, oily rag out of her mouth. There was no way ingesting that stuff was good.

She grimaced. "Water."

Deva looked around, then ran over to a small fridge, which had several bottles inside. Once Carol had some of the water to drink, she looked up at us with wide, terrified eyes. "This is so much worse than we ever imagined."

TWENTY-SIX

Emma

"What happened?" Deva asked.

Carol opened her mouth, then shook her head, pure pain written across her face.

"Let's just get her out of here first," I said, scared. I'd never seen her like this before.

Carol let her head thump back against the wall of the office, and I told my back that this was a time to be strong as I knelt down, wrapped one of my arms around her waist, and put one of her arms around my shoulders.

"Easy does it." I pretty much held Carol up as she struggled to get on her feet. Deva and I helped her to the car and into the backseat while Beth watched our backs. Carol was definitely more banged up than she'd looked at first.

"I... tried... to escape," she gritted out. "He blasted me... across the garage."

Anger rolled through me. "Well, he's going to pay for that."

And, oh boy, this guy was going to pay for a lot of things. As my mind went through everything we knew, and Joel became the culprit for every bad event connected with that symbol, my parent's accident, and Sarah and Thomas's accident, my anger grew and grew.

Who was this sick guy? And why had he done so many terrible things?

"I think I have... broken ribs," she hissed as she finally relaxed in my backseat. Relaxed may be the wrong word, but she wasn't quite as tense as she had been before. Broken ribs were no joke though. If one of them punctured her lung I'd never forgive myself for not getting to her in time.

These women, my best friends, the people who knew me better than anyone else, had become more important to me than I thought possible. It wasn't just that our friendships had been revived when I came back to Mystic Hollow, they'd been strengthened as well. The bonds we had could never be broken, no matter what. And no one would ever get in the way of our sisterhood ever again.

"Do you think he's still here?" I asked her.

Talking seemed to cost her because she gritted out the word, "no."

As I tucked Carol's feet into the car pain was written all over her face and I gave her a tight-lipped smile before I said, "We'll get you taken care of, just hang in there."

She nodded and I shut the door as gently as I could, so it didn't jostle Carol unnecessarily.

"We need to do a sweep of the place," I said to Deva and Beth.

Deva gave a grim nod. "Beth, you stay with Carol for a minute while we check the place over."

Beth agreed, and Deva and I carefully swept through the place. There was so much damage. Way more than would have come from throwing Joel across the shop. There had been a fight. And as I stopped at the claw mark on the door, I had a terrible feeling.

"Could this be Daniel?"

Deva looked at it. "Maybe. But it doesn't mean it was from today."

"Was this where his car was being fixed?"

Deva stiffened. "Probably."

Damn it. None of this was good.

I called Daniel. Again. And again. I sent him a text begging him to call me, and then we double checked the place. There were definitely no signs of Daniel or Joel. I wasn't sure if that was a good thing or a bad thing.

We went back outside before racing out to the car. I got into the driver's seat while Deva jumped into the passenger seat beside me. I turned on the engine, then hesitated. We needed to find Daniel. But right now, Carol needed help.

"I think... I think I'm going to pass out," Carol whispered, and her words were almost a sob.

I felt sick. The hospital was a good thirty-minute drive, and Carol's keys were nowhere to be found to run back to the library to get hers, so there was no time to waste. I was worried about Daniel, but Carol needed me right now.

My heart was hammering in my chest the whole ride. I didn't want to push Carol further after all she'd been through, but we needed answers or more people could get hurt.

Or die.

"What did you figure out at the library? Do you know what Joel is up to?" I asked. This drive wasn't going to be easy, there were lots of winding curves in the road and though I wanted to speed through them to get us there as quickly as possible, I couldn't. At least, not without jerking

Carol about and causing her more pain. As my mom would say, "More haste, less speed."

I must have mumbled it to myself because I felt Deva's hand on my arm as she reached over from the passenger seat. When I glanced at her she gave me a tight-lipped smile and squeezed my arm before mouthing the words, "You've got this."

I nodded and sped up as much as I was comfortable doing.

"Joel is human," Carol said after a moment of getting settled down in the seat and used to the movement of the car, her head now rested in Beth's lap. "But he learned dark magic and tricked your parents, and others, into helping him perform a spell that would supposedly protect you. But really it was a spell that helped him live longer and gave him powers."

"What the hell?" I whispered. "Gave him powers? I didn't think that kind of thing was possible."

Carol was quiet for a moment. "I'm not sure. He rambled a lot, telling me about this stuff in spurts. He's super angry. Like, really angry. I gather things aren't going the way he wanted." After sucking in a shuddering breath, she continued. "The best I got from his tirades was that the spell was supposed to protect him from anyone knowing what he did, but your parents remembered. The car accident was because they didn't forget."

A lump formed in my throat. My parents had been murdered. It was official. I knew they'd said that the accident we were all in wasn't an accident, but that didn't make me feel any better. This whole time only Joel had known. How was that fair? How could they have rested peacefully if no one knew that they were murdered? If no one was looking for their killer?

An iron will formed within me and I knew without a doubt that come hell or high water I'd find Joel and I'd make sure he could never hurt anyone again. I wasn't sure that I could make him pay for his crimes, even with my powers as karma, but I'd give it my best shot.

"Over time, the spell weakened, so he did it again when we were in high school. That's what Daniel's wife got mixed up in. But she remembered. Just like your parents. And so, he was going to kill her, too. And he realized she'd told Thomas."

"So, he got rid of Thomas and Sarah in one go. Did the same thing to my parents," I whispered, horrified. "And nobody else caught on, not all that time."

"He needs to do the spell again since apparently it only keeps him young and powerful for a while. He's found some humans and supernatural people to help him with it." She tried to sit up. Something about what she needed to say made her feel like she needed to move and that made my stomach clench. Whatever she was about to tell us I knew it wasn't good. We all did.

When she gasped, I glanced at her in the rearview mirror and saw that she'd gone pale and was clutching her side again. Whatever she'd done it had hurt her ribs even more. I couldn't help but look back at her again when there was nothing but silence from the backseat for a moment. Her lower lip trembled, and her eyes glistened with unshed tears. It made me press down on the gas pedal and hurry even more. I hated that my friend was in pain. I could almost feel it reverberating through the car like she was channeling it outward.

"Don't try to sit up. Don't strain yourself or you could make it worse," Deva said, turning to look at her. "What is it?"

A tiny sob escaped Carol before she said, "Emma, he's got Henry and his online friends helping him. He's been working on them for months through that game they play. I'm so sorry."

Henry? No!

"And Daniel?" I asked, his name almost a sob.

"Daniel came to check his office. I think he suspected something. When he saw me, Joel attacked him from behind. I heard a big fight and then Daniel's truck start. I wanted to see what happened, but I couldn't."

Daniel and Henry. Two of the most important people in my life... I couldn't lose them like I lost my parents. This cycle of death and loss by this jackass had to end.

And we were going to be the ones to end it.

She went quiet after that. All the energy seemed to have been sapped from her and I couldn't blame her. After everything she'd been through and the amount of pain, she was in it was no wonder that she'd finally passed out. She'd told us what she needed to and with that task done her body finally told her enough was enough.

So, I called the sheriff. "Hey!"

"Listen, we're still trying to find the kids. Is this important?" he barked, his voice coming in and out over the bad connection.

My heart raced. "Joel Northman is the one who killed Al. And he's killed others. And he's about to kill again... my brother, Daniel, and some other people."

"Shit!" His voice came out crackled. "We have a damned serial killer in Mystic Hollow! And all the cops are stuck deep in the woods tracking down idiot kids. I'll send help when I can."

I hoped the help would come sooner rather than later.

"Thanks. Until then, we'll do what we can."

"I knew you would," he said, a knowing tone to his voice.

We pulled in at the ER, and I stopped the car right in front of the doors, trying to give as little distance that Carol had to walk as possible.

"I can take her," Beth said. "You guys save Henry and Daniel."

"Thank you," I said, trying not to cry as she helped Carol from the car.

Luckily, a couple nurses were outside with a stretcher in seconds. My heart ached as I watched them wheel her into the hospital, with Beth racing after them.

"Please, let her be okay."

"She's tough," Deva said, reaching out and squeezing my hand.

She is.

I shifted the car into gear. As much as I wanted to focus on Beth, we had some murders to stop.

TWENTY-SEVEN

Emma

WE TOOK a gamble and headed to my house, since Henry said his group was meeting there, with Deva beside me performing a tracker spell. She said it was tricky, but easier with someone she knew, so she was hoping to be able to figure out where Henry was, and thought it'd lead us to Joel. My chest ached with every mile that passed. Maybe we were heading in the wrong direction. Maybe Joel had had them all meet somewhere in the middle of nowhere.

We really had no idea. All I knew was that I'd tried calling Henry and Daniel over and over again, and neither of them had answered.

Neither of them. It made me want to just start bawling then and there.

Finally, Deva dropped her hands from her head and said, "Henry is definitely still at your house. I can feel him very strongly."

Thank goodness!

Then, she grabbed her phone and started texting rapidly.

I frowned. "Although it's convenient Henry's meeting with his whole group tonight at our place for the first time..."

"You think Joel has his hands in that too?" Deva asked, frowning.

"I wouldn't put it past that snake."

The *murderer*.

A man who had killed my parents, leaving Henry and I without our family, and performed some kind of spell on a little girl to get what he wanted. Who'd killed Thomas and Sarah and broken Daniel's heart. And left a boy without his father. And kidnapped and hurt Carol and Daniel.

Oh, yeah, this guy was going to pay!

As we pulled onto my street, I saw cars parked all over. These must have been Henry's gamer friends. And then, I spotted Daniel's truck blocking the cars in my driveway.

Damn it. If Daniel could drive, he would have called me. Joel must have taken his truck and brought it here. The monster was inside with my brother, some innocent people, and probably Daniel.

My skin crawled. If he hurt them, Karma would go crazy.

Even now, I felt my powers growing under my skin. If I was sure from this distance, and without seeing my target, it would work, I'd let it go. I would release my magic like a storm and hope that it found Joel and made him pay.

But I couldn't gamble with the lives of the two most important men in my life.

I was about to face down a man who had taken down my parents, two shifters, *and* my bear. As much as I wanted to believe my powers would be enough, I wasn't sure. But I *had* to be sure we could win against Joel. Losing would destroy me.

As soon as we parked, I turned to Deva, knowing what we needed to do. "Take my car, go get the coven. Get back here as fast as you can."

"You're not going in there alone!" Deva exclaimed, looking at me like I'd lost my mind.

"Deva--"

"Besides, I already texted the coven as we drove."

I was shocked. She hated working with the coven, which meant she must realize how bad this situation was.

"Thanks, Deva," I whispered.

And we both climbed out of the car and ran for the door.

"Here." She dug a couple of wrapped candies out of her purse. "I keep these in my pocket for emergencies. These will make you..." She waved her hand, trying to find the word. "Stronger, better. More capable? They're just intended to make you a more powerful you." She put one in my hand, then grabbed my wrist before I popped the caramel-colored candy into my mouth. "They're strong."

As soon as I swallowed the first mouthful of caramel flavoring, my body quivered. But then, half a second later, it settled. I felt... mostly normal, just a slight tingling in my stomach, like I'd eaten something that didn't quite agree with me. I hoped the candies were really as strong as she'd said.

We needed all the help we could get.

We went into the house as quietly as possible to find Henry sitting in the living room playing his video game, unhurt. A wave of relief moved through me as my gaze moved around the room. He wasn't the only one playing a video game. Four other guys focused solely on the screen while Joel Northman himself sat in the recliner, staring at me and Deva. "Hello," Joel said, a smirk twisting his lips. "I've been waiting for you."

Well, that's not creepy at all.

I glanced from Joel to Henry, who seemed to realize we'd come in. "Hey, sis." He paused their game and looked from me to Joel, then jumped slightly. "When did you get a gun, Joel?"

Inching forward, I saw what he was talking about. Joel had a gun on his lap... pointed right at Henry. "Don't move, any of you."

The rest of the men playing the game figured out something was wrong in an instant. Each of them settled back against the chair or sofa they sat in, wide-eyed and paling fast. "What's going on?" one of them asked.

"What's going on," Joel drawled, "is that Daniel is chained to something heavy, just out your back door, in the water. And the tide is coming in. *Fast*. Now, what I plan for Henry and his friends won't kill them. But Daniel? Even that old bear can't survive underwater..." He lifted a brow, letting his words settle over the room. "Now, you have to understand, I don't want to hurt anyone. And I know what you can do. So, I'm giving you the chance to rescue Daniel, while I do what I do, or to stay here and let him die. Up to you."

My instinct was to go after Daniel, but Joel had a gun on my brother. What in the world was I supposed to do?

"Is this... is this the guy who killed mom and dad?" Henry asked.

I hesitated, worried he might do something dangerous, but then nodded. My brother needed to know just how grave a situation we were in.

"Go," Henry said, and there was a look on his face I'd never seen before. "I know what to do."

"Yeah," Deva echoed, a dangerous note to her voice. "Get Daniel. I won't let Henry get hurt."

I tried to blast Joel with my power of Karma, so that maybe his gun would backfire and explode in his hand or something, but nothing happened. Instead, Joel flinched and looked angrier.

"Trying your powers on me?" he smirked. "Sorry, but this won't be that easy. Now, yes, eventually you might be able to hurt me. But you have to ask yourself, do you have the *time?*"

"If you so much as--"

Joel cut me off. "He's going to drown if you're too late. Better hurry."

I looked back at Henry.

His eyes said to trust me. That he wasn't scared. But I was. This was my little brother.

"Go," Deva whispered.

Moaning in frustration, I took off running, tearing through the living room, throwing open the back doors, and running down the porch steps. Thankfully, I'd put my sneakers on this morning, and they helped me launch through the sand as fast as I could. Even so, my lungs were burning, and I felt like I was moving backwards in the sand, as my gaze roamed over the ocean, looking for any sign of him.

"Daniel!" I screamed. He could've been anywhere up and down this stretch of beach, assuming Joel was even telling the truth.

Again, I tried to pull on my power. It didn't want to work, though. "Come on," I moaned as I ran, praying I was headed in the right direction. "Daniel!"

And then, there he was. Way too far out, and barely keeping his head above the water. A particularly high wave crested and broke and he went under.

I bounded into the water, running as fast as I could, lifting my feet high, praying fervently there were no undertows. "I'm coming!"

As I moved, I practically begged my powers to work. I felt completely helpless, knowing I'd left Deva and Henry, not to mention those random guys, back at my house. Who knew if they'd be able to defend themselves against him?

But I couldn't even focus on that because Daniel was dying in front of me. Faster than I could swim. Every time a wave crashed over him, his expression got more and more frantic, and his gasps for air got worse.

It got to where I couldn't touch the bottom of the ocean floor, and as I began to swim, I caught Daniel's gaze for just a moment. His expression said it all. He said goodbye, and that it was okay. All with just one look.

Then, a wave crested over him. And when it drew back, I couldn't see any more of him. He was underwater, running out of air, and I was too far away.

I swam with all my might, my limbs shaking, fighting against the current that seemed to want to keep me from saving my bear's life. But no matter how much I pushed myself, all I could see was the spot Daniel had disappeared and felt the seconds until he ran out of air ticking away.

No! No, I did not accept that. He was a good man. He'd done so much for this town, and constantly did things for others. He'd suffered several tragedies and he did *not* deserve to go out like this!

My powers flared to life as the desperation inside me crested. I felt the tingling spread over my body. I smelled something for a moment that was reassuring and warm, like

Daniel, or like smores being cooked over a fireplace, and knew my magic was responding. And then, a ripple shot out from me in the water, expanding out in every direction.

It *felt* like power. Like something stronger than even the ocean.

Daniel surged above the water, not just his head peeking above the waves, but his head and shoulders. And I knew, instinctively, or maybe magically, that his chain had snapped.

He was free.

I swam harder, but I wasn't just swimming to reach Daniel, I was taking the steps to get back to Joel... and destroy him for everything he'd done.

TWENTY-EIGHT

Emma

Daniel suddenly shifted into a huge bear. He barreled toward me, swimming in the water faster than I ever imagined possible. One second, I was struggling, and then he was beside me. He pressed against me, and I grabbed the fur on his back, and then we were surging toward the shore.

It was hard to see around him, but I knew the instant his feet could touch the bottom of the ocean floor. We moved faster, and after a minute, I slid from his back and struggled the rest of the way to the shore.

Only, we weren't alone out on the beach.

I looked up to find Henry, the four guys he'd been playing with, and Deva standing with their hands up in front of Joel and his gun. "So, you managed it," Joel said with a laugh. "Now I can kill the bear, too. He'll just make my spell stronger."

Kill? I knew the monster was blowing smoke when he said he didn't want to hurt anyone.

"You're pretty cocky," I shouted, coming closer and closer as my bear growled behind me.

"I have a reason to be," he said, leveling his gun at me. "And when all this is over, I'll be even more powerful, and you'll all be dead."

"Not if we have anything to do with it." Khat, the leader of the coven, stepped out from around the side of our house. Joel turned sideways and waved the gun back and forth, from me and Daniel-bear, to Deva and Henry, to the coven. Carol and Beth were right behind them, with a temporary brace on Carol's wrist. Apparently, her ribs weren't the only thing she'd injured.

Khat held out a hand, but then her brow furrowed when nothing happened.

Joel laughed cruelly. "Oh, yeah, about that. The spell lets me suck the power away from those nearest me. I'm just drawing your power in right now, and you're not able to use them." He looked so proud. I wanted to wipe the smirk off of his damn face. "And once I kill you, I keep your power forever. That was my mistake before. Thinking I could leave my sources alive. But with them alive, my powers fade. This time, I won't make the same mistake. If I kill you, your powers will be mine *forever*."

He turned his gun toward Henry. "You first."

No! I had to slow Joel down.

"Why us?" I called across the sand, trying not to sound desperate as a plan formed in my mind. "Why me and Henry and our parents?"

"Your parents?" He shrugged like killing them was nothing at all. "Circumstance. It just happened that they lived here at a time when I learned how to take powers. They were convenient. And Sarah... it was her bleeding heart. Her naiveté that she could help protect the people she cared for. But Henry..." With a slightly unhinged laugh, he scratched his temple with his gun. "He was easy. I was able to manipulate him through the game. I put together a team of *special* humans and supernaturals, knowing that it would be too easy. And then when I heard Emma had moved back into town, I figured, hey. It was time to redo my spell, anyway. Might as well get the massive powers of Karma." His smile spread as he glanced back at me. "I look forward to taking care of you last. How delicious that will be."

Everyone stared at him as if they were focusing. Deva, Carol, the entire coven. The group of a dozen or so women, some young, some older, were all focused on the man. As if crazy gun-wielding men threatened them every day, and that nothing would stop them from whatever magic they were preparing to unleash on him.

I just hoped focusing was enough to get through whatever ability he had. But I wasn't banking on that. Instead, I slowly inched backwards in the sand. Karma's powers had worked out in the water. How far did I have to get away from him before they worked again?

"Nothing?" Joel asked, scanning all of us as if disappointed.

My thoughts scrambled as I continued to inch backward. I needed to buy some time. "So, you're basically just a human who became a thief?"

His smile faded. "Do you have any idea how difficult it is for a human to wield black magic? What we have to do... what we have to become... to force magic into us? It's like growing another organ, Emma, my dear." He shook his head as if remembering dark things. "Some humans have a piece of it inside of themselves. Coaxing it to life isn't hard. Some have a wealth of magic but lack the ability to access it. I had neither. Nothing. Not even a spark inside of myself."

"Maybe that was for a reason," I said, having to speak louder as I created space between us.

He glared. "The *reason* is that the world isn't fair, but that I've found a way to make it fair."

"No--" I began, followed by another step back

"Enough! I know you're trying to give those witches time to break through my abilities. But I lied before. My abilities don't have weaknesses or limitations. The witches could have forever, and still couldn't defeat me." He leveled the gun at me. "But you inching away? Sorry, sweetheart, but that's not going to be allowed to happen. It was a clever idea, but I'm far smarter. So, now, it's time. Your time. Just be glad you won't have to watch me kill your loved ones."

Daniel lumbered forward with a roar, stepping between me and danger, but Joel simply swung his barrel toward the giant bear. "I guess I'll have to start with you instead. I'll absorb your extra potent life energy, but no magic, not from a shifter." He shrugged. "At least I get to kill you."

"No!" I screamed, wanting to go forward, but instead taking several big steps back in desperation.

Daniel roared again and then started racing at Joel... like he could be faster than a bullet.

As Joel pulled the trigger, my heart squeezed with more pain than I'd ever felt. Not since my parents died. Not even with Rick. It was like a sizzling over my body, like I was on fire.

I would not lose Daniel.

"I will *not*." My voice filled the air as my power exploded out of me.

And exactly as I'd envisioned earlier, the gun in his hand malfunctioned. No bullet came. Instead, there was just a puff of smoke.

Daniel took the opportunity to barrel into Joel, knocking

him back on the sand. Then, Daniel settled down on Joel as Deva grabbed Carol and Beth's hands. The coven circled them. "We're siphoning off his power now," Khat called. "He'll be a normal human soon."

"Just don't move!" Deva added, pointing at Daniel.

The big bear just chuffed. I suspected he wasn't putting his full weight on the squirming and screaming Joel, either.

I wanted to move closer, but then Deva looked back at me. "Has Karma done whatever it's going to do?"

The truth was I didn't know. A gun not going off was hardly Karmic justice, but the power I'd felt moments before had to have done more than that. It'd felt like a wave that exploded from me out to all of Mystic Hollow.

"I think so," I shouted, then pushed my legs through the waves to reach shore.

I circled as the coven continued murmuring and knelt near Joel's head. "What about Al?" I asked. "And Thomas?"

Joel stopped screaming in anger and glared at me. "They... got in the way." And then his eyes narrowed. "No matter what happens, I'm not done. No one can stop me. And you've made a very powerful enemy."

I leaned closer with a smile that was all teeth. "*You've* made a very powerful enemy."

Daniel shifted and Joel made a pathetic pained sound under his weight. "You... have no idea. Still... so clueless. All of you."

I frowned. Clueless about what?

"You can get up," Deva told Daniel. "We're done. He's human again."

Daniel shifted back and hauled Joel up, so he sat on the beach. "Don't move," he growled, naked, massive, and scary as hell.

"I hear sirens," Deva shouted.

I nodded. "I let them know what was happening."

But that wasn't my focus now. Joel was.

"I'm still so confused," I said, almost to myself. "What made you go after me and my family?"

Joel smiled. "Why not?"

Daniel punched him square in the face. Joel smacked back onto the beach, then turned his head and spit out blood, before slowly sitting back up.

"Answer her question," Daniel growled.

Joely wasn't smiling any longer. "You can hit me all you want, bear. She'll never know the truth. None of you will."

My teeth made a sound as they clacked together. "Can you guys do a spell to make him talk?"

Khat grinned. "Sort of." She bent over and got in his face. "Tell the truth or I'll make your dick shrivel up and fall off. You'll have a pee hole sticking out of your FUPA."

Joel swallowed audibly. "You wouldn't."

She waved her hand and started to repeat a spell.

He screamed and grabbed at his crotch. "Stop! I'll talk! I'll talk!"

Khat dropped her hand. "Better talk fast."

Joel was shaking, still clenching his crotch, like it could save his dick. "I came across a spell to make me live forever when I learned about supernaturals in high school. It took time to figure out how to execute it, but I did, and then I found two victims to try it out on. I stole Emma's parents' powers when we were in school together before they even realized that they weren't just human."

My parents... they weren't human? Then what were they?

"Years passed, and I could feel my strength fading. I knew I needed to find someone else for the spell, and I sensed magic in Henry and Emma. I thought because my spell had worked on their parents so easily, that it would work as easily on their kids. I could take what I wanted from the kids, and their parents would never know."

"And?" I asked, feeling outraged for all he'd done to my family.

"I convinced them all over again that there were dangerous supernaturals in the world and that the spell was the only way to protect their kids. They fell for it, and I performed the spell on both of you."

We had powers too? Wouldn't we know if we'd had powers?

Joel continued more slowly. "I also performed the memory spell on your parents. But this time, something went wrong. They started to remember."

"So, you killed them," I growled.

He shrugged. "But then my magic continued to weaken, and I had to perform the spell again. I coaxed Sarah into it, thinking that using a shifter this time might help me retain the powers I stole. But it didn't. And what was worse, the memory spell didn't seem to work as well on a paranormal."

"And that's when Sarah figured it out," Deva said.

Joel nodded. "And the bitch had to tell someone, so I had to take out the wolf alpha, too."

"Thomas," Daniel said in a deep, threatening voice. He lunged forward, but I grabbed his arm.

I couldn't have physically stopped him in a million years, but he halted as if I were strong enough. "Let him finish. It'll be our last chance to ask questions since he'll be going to jail for a long time."

"That's all there is to say," Joel answered, eyeing Daniel with fear. "The spell worked, until recently, so I got Al's help to set up a trap to steal Emma's powers once more. Only, all the work I'd done convincing Al that you were just pure evil and deserved it all for what you'd done to your ex. He snooped around. Leaving notes. Watching you. And then he started to doubt you were really as bad as I said, so he had to be dealt with and my plan had to be moved up..." He shrugged.

The sound of sirens coming down our street, and then officers talking hit us.

I wrapped my arms around Daniel's waist. I couldn't look at Joel for another minute. "He's going to jail for the rest of his hopefully short life," I said. "We will have justice for our families."

"It won't just be jail," Daniel said in a strangely knowing voice. "That wouldn't be enough. If Karma has come for him, I know he'll experience every moment of suffering, loss, and pain we ever felt." His voice cracked on the words.

And then, we were holding each other tightly.

Daniel buried his face into my hair, and his shoulders shook. I was shaking too. It wasn't enough that we'd lost the people we loved so long ago, we had uncovered terrible stories of betrayal, lies, and cruelty. It hurt all over again.

And yet, this time I wasn't alone, trying to care for Henry as he grieved. Daniel and I were a team. Partners. More than just that though. In each other, we had a hope that with all this death and destruction, something beautiful could emerge.

"It's over," I whispered, stroking my hands through his hair.

Maybe the unhappy spirits, strange messages, and dead bodies were over. But as I heard the cops approaching, I knew that this was only the end to one chapter in our lives.

I hoped the next one was better.

TWENTY-NINE

Emma

"Feel better," I said. "Tell Deva to make you extra brownies."

Carol chuckled as she hung up. I'd called to check on her before bed. She had a broken wrist and bruised ribs, but she'd get better. Beth and Deva were working to help her heal faster, which was an even bigger relief. Magic was an amazing thing when you knew how to use it, but it wasn't an instant cure-all.

It'd been a week since we sent Joel to prison. As a human, now without powers, he'd spend his life in jail as a serial killer. The prosecution had plenty of evidence of what he'd done, they'd just have to keep the magic part out of it. And if Joel brought it up... well, he'd go to a secure psychiatric facility. I wasn't sure which I thought would be the better punishment, but I knew Karma would take care of it. My powers always seemed to know what to do and when, even if I had to nudge them occasionally.

I sighed and turned over, snuggling closer to Daniel. "I'm glad you're here," I said.

He hadn't left my side since we watched Joel being carted away, and I was not arguing with it. With his gaze locked onto mine, Daniel lowered his face toward me until I had to close my eyes or cross them. And then his lips took away all of my senses.

In one instant I was surrounded by everything Daniel, like I'd been plucked from the real world and dropped into this sensory overload. The scent of the forest was embedded in him along with a scent that was strictly his own and very masculine. The stubble on his face rubbed against my own as his lips caressed mine. It wasn't unpleasant, in fact, I quite liked the juxtaposition of soft and textured. The feel of his skin and t-shirt under my fingers made me itch to pull the fabric up and expose the rest of him.

The longer he kissed me the more I wanted him to kiss me and the more I wanted him in general. I hadn't felt like this in years, and it honestly made me feel like a teenager again, making out in my bedroom, parents telling me to leave the door open. I had actual butterflies in my stomach as his hands gripped me tighter and pulled me closer. It was like we couldn't get enough of one another. Something I only thought young people experienced when it came to new relationships, turned out it didn't matter the age.

His tongue swiped against the seam of my lips, and I opened for him. As soon as he began devouring me, he let out a deep, rumbly groan that had my insides quivering with anticipation. He tasted like mouthwash and even that sent a thrill through me since that meant that he'd gotten ready for bed here, with me.

I hooked my leg over his hip so I could press myself closer and there was a rumple of approval from him as he broke away from my mouth and began to kiss my neck. My head tipped back of its own accord, giving him access to pretty much anything he wanted. If I was younger, I might have been worried about how I looked at that moment, was I sexy enough? Now, I was comfortable enough in my own skin that I knew if he was here with me then he wanted me and I didn't need to second guess that, just appreciate it for what it was.

Just as Daniel's hand slid under my shirt, heading upward toward my breasts, my doorbell rang. Henry was gone to Alice's house, so there wasn't anyone else to answer the door.

I moaned and Daniel rolled away. "Seriously?" he gasped. "It's eleven at night."

"Come on," I grumbled. "Go with me. This late, it's probably the police here to ask more questions about Joel."

He shuffled behind me out into the hallway and down the stairs. When I opened the door, I realized I couldn't have been more wrong.

A pale, tall man stood on my porch. He had a bit of a paunch and his hair had seen thicker days, but he was handsome, with intense blue eyes rimmed by red. He also hummed with strength, which instantly had me on guard. Was he human?

"Hello," he said, seeming a little shy and uncertain. "I'm Bryan... and I need Karma's help."

Daniel put his arm in front of me and sort of shoved me backward, putting himself in between me and Bryan. "What are you doing here?" And there was anger in his voice.

Anger? Why? Who was this?

The man held up his hand. "I come in peace. I really do need her help."

"What's going on?" I asked.

"He's a vampire," Daniel snarled. "A blood sucker." He may as well have spit on the floor for the venom in his voice.

"I'm also Carol's ex-boyfriend," Bryan said slowly, as if he wasn't sure whether his words would help or hurt him.

Oh! I peered around Daniel again. I had just recently seen his picture in a yearbook. Time had definitely changed him. But not as much as I would have thought. I guess that was to be expected with a vampire though. He still had a little bit of softness to his face, like a young man, but a few wrinkles on his forehead and beside his eyes. His shoulders were strong, even though his overall frame was on the thinner side.

I had a feeling if he was smiling, I would have instantly recognized him for who he was.

"You're the Bryan who left her without even a good-bye?" I asked, shocked. Though as soon as it passed my curiosity roared to life.

He nodded and shrugged. "And now you know why."

Because he'd become a vampire? I betted there was a whole story there, and I hoped it could justify why he'd broken my friend's heart. Otherwise, he might not find Karma so much of a help, as the boot that was going to kick his butt with justice.

With a sigh, I tugged on Daniel's arm. "Is the old vampire thing true?" I asked. "About inviting them in?"

He shook his head. "No. He could force his way in if he wanted to."

Well, there was no point in him having to stand on the porch. "Come on in, Bryan. Tell me what's going on. But start by telling me how you knew I was Karma."

He started talking before he even crossed the threshold. "Well, as for that, everyone in the supernatural world knows

Karma handed down her mantle. We all knew who the old Karma was, too, but she made herself hard to find, unlike you. Don't be surprised if you get a lot of attention if you don't go into hiding. Everyone wants to get what they think they deserve." The last bit sounded more like he was complaining about someone else.

It was the first part that stuck in my mind. More attention was exactly what I *didn't* need. It wasn't like the police thought I was a magnet for trouble already or anything...

"As for what's going on?" He continued. "I've been going through my uncle's stuff and found out that there's something really bad going on in Mystic Hollow."

"Your uncle?" I asked, unsure who he was related to. I swear my brain had a limited capacity for facts and just randomly deleted stuff, so instead of forgetting things like state capitals when I learned something new, I'd forget things like who Bryan's uncle was, even though I felt sure I knew at some point.

"Cliff Miller. I came back for his funeral."

"Oh my god. I'm so sorry!"

Cliff was the terrible lawyer who had been Beth's ex's business partner. What her ex had done to him, just to steal their business was cruel, but the monster he'd become couldn't just be ignored. As in I, or my karma powers, had turned Cliff into a rat. I guess him missing for so long had been enough for him to be officially declared dead, which had brought Bryan here.

"Are you doing okay?" I asked because I didn't know what else to say. If he wanted Karma to handle who took out his uncle, he might be in for a surprise.

"I'm okay. We weren't actually that close," Bryan replied. "The important thing is that we're all in big trouble."

Trouble. Darn it. Trouble was something I had some experience with.

"Better tell us the whole story, and go slowly, we've had a few rough weeks..."

GET ready to read Karma's Stake, book 4 of Magical Midlife in Mystic Hollow! Preorder it here.

Court of Midnight

The Hollow

(Cowritten with Ellabee Andrews)

Survival

Seduction

Surrender

Salsang Chronicles

(cowritten with Serena Akeroyd)

Stained Egos

Stained Hearts

Stained Minds

Stained Bonds

Stained Souls

Salsang Chronicles Box Set

Cerberus

Daughter of Persephone

Daughter of Hades

Queen of the Underworld

Cerberus Series Box Set

Hera's Gift (A Cerberus Series Novella)

Four Worlds

Wounding Atlantis

Finding Hyperborea

Escaping El Dorado

Embracing Agartha – Coming Soon

Wardens of Midnight

Woman of Midnight (A Wardens of Midnight Novella)

Sanctuary at Midnight

The Siren Legacy

The Oracle (A Siren Legacy Novella)

The Siren's Son

The Siren's Eyes

The Siren's Code

The Siren's Heart

The Banshee (A Siren Legacy Novella)

The Siren's Bride

Fury's Valentine (A Siren Legacy Novella)

Standalones, Shared Worlds, and Box Sets

The Sex Tape

Spin My Gold (Cowritten with Lacey Carter Andersen)

Buttercup

Neve

ALSO BY L.A. BORUFF

Prime Time of Life https://laboruff.com/books/primetime-of-life/
Borrowed Time
Stolen Time
Just in Time

GIRDLES AND GHOULS HTTPS://WWW.BOOKS2READ.COM/GIRDLES

WITCHING AFTER FORTY HTTPS://LABORUFF.COM/BOOKS/WITCHING-AFTER-FORTY/
A Ghoulish Midlife
Cookies For Satan (A Christmas Story)
I'm With Cupid (A Valentine's Day Story)
A Cursed Midlife
Feeding Them Won't Make Them Grow (A Birthday Story)

A Girlfriend For Mr. Snoozleton (A Girlfriend Story)
A Haunting Midlife
An Animated Midlife
A Killer Midlife

FANGED   AFTER   FORTY   HTTPS://WWW.
BOOKS2READ.COM/FANGED1
Bitten in the Midlife

MAGICAL   MIDLIFE   **in Mystic Hollow**   https://
laboruff.com/books/mystic-hollow/
Karma's Spell
Karma's Shift
Karma's Spirit

SHIFTING   INTO   MIDLIFE   HTTPS://
LABORUFF.COM/BOOKS/SHIFTING-INTO-
MIDLIFE/
Pack Bunco Night

ABOUT THE AUTHOR

Helen Scott lives in the Chicago area with her wonderful husband and furry, four-legged kids. She spends way too much time with her nose in a book and isn't sorry about it. When not reading or writing, Helen can be found absorbed in one video game or another or crafting her heart out.

Thank you for reading!
You can also come and hang out in my reader group, Helen's Hellraisers, where you can find out all about what I'm working on, sneak peeks, and even exclusive giveaways! Come and join the fun here!
Don't want to join the group but want to know what's going on?
Follow me on social media:
Website: http://www.helenscottauthor.com
Facebook: http://www.facebook.com/helenscottauthor/
Twitter: http://twitter.com/HelenM459
Instagram: http://www.instagram.com/helenscottauthor/
Don't forget to sign up for my newsletter for new release alerts, giveaways, and other fun stuff!

ABOUT THE AUTHOR

Lacey Carter writes paranormal women's fiction and cozy mysteries with humor, adventure, and a little romance. Her stories are sure to make you smile, laugh, and maybe even cry. But don't worry, she's always sure to give her readers a happy ending for her brave heroes and heroines.

As a USA Today bestselling author, Lacey is always working on another story. She thrives off of the adventure both in her books and outside of them, while raising her three beautiful children, with her amazing husband. She also writes steamy romances under the name Lacey Carter Andersen.

So if you're looking for fun and adventure, dive into one of her worlds today!

ABOUT THE AUTHOR

L.A. (Lainie) Boruff lives in East Tennessee with her husband, three children, and an ever growing number of cats. She loves reading, watching TV, and procrastinating by browsing Facebook. L.A.'s passions include vampires, food, and listening to heavy metal music. She once won a Harry Potter trivia contest based on the books and lost one based on the movies. She has two bands on her bucket list that she still hasn't seen: AC/DC and Alice Cooper. Feel free to send tickets.